Janna Hoag was raised in
dissimilar to the Adams Family ⸻ ⸺ school to double
as a hand and foot model for catalogues at the studio where
she worked as a graphic artist.

At home with young children she began freelancing, writing
for comics, women's and teen magazines; doing a stint as
agony aunt on one of them. Later she ran art and drama
groups and had thirteen children's books published.

Drawn into fringe theatre in Manchester, several of her
plays have been workshopped and one of them toured
professionally. This is her first novel.

Janna Hoag

A LITTLE PALACE

This novel was joint winner of the Crocus North West Novel Competition in 1999, judged by Livi Michael, Danny Peak and Karline Smith.

First published in 2000 by Crocus
Crocus books are published by Commonword Ltd, Cheetwood House, 21 Newton Street, Manchester M1 1FZ.

Commonword gratefully acknowledges financial assistance from the Association of Greater Manchester Authorities, Manchester City Council and North West Arts Board.

Crocus Books are distributed by Turnaround Publisher Services Ltd, Unit 3, Olympia Trading Estate, Coburg Road, Wood Green, London N22 6TZ.

Cover illustration by Janna Hoag.
Cover design by Ian Bobb.

Printed by Seddon Printers, Unit 6 Kay Works, Moor Lane, Bolton BL1 4TH.

British Library Cataloguing-in-Publication Data. A catalogue record for this book is available from British Library.

To Michael I. Elphick

for all his help

CHAPTER ONE

'Rick, why aren't you finished?' bawled Alb Wakes to the shivering girl perched at the top of the ladder.

She frowned at the pink sorbet sky then down at her tormentor. She aimed the pigeon, imagining the splat as it hit him in the face, shards of beak up his nose. A moment earlier her fingers had sunk in the rotted corpse as she scooped gobbets of muck from the gutters of St. Chad's, a job she'd slogged at for an hour, having first done the church hall and Scout hut. The textures of animal and vegetable slime were disgusting, her hands raw with filth, nails cracked. Yet she preferred to suffer this than get his lecture if he saw she'd forgotten rubber gloves. He'd use the opportunity to tell her, yet again, she was a useless lump, a drain on his resources. She was sick of being called 'a horrible little man'.

'I'm on the last bit, Dad.'

'Then help Bernard with the fencing. The ends of the staves need sharpening. Here's the axe.'

Erica glanced across the car park. Under a clump of leafless trees the figure of her sister, Bernardine, moved rhythmically in the gloom, sawing branches to section part of the area into a playground for the crèche. This sprucing up was their father's latest scheme to remind the neighbourhood what a treasure he was. What Erica thought of as buffing his tin-pot halo. He'd made her and her sisters work at the current project for a month, every weekend and most evenings in spite of arctic temperatures. He'd started today's work party at six a.m. when it was dark, apart from distant street lamps, a problem he solved by switching on all the lights of the hall and opening the double doors.

Albert Wakes had his image fine tuned to a point approaching sainthood. Outside the family he was referred to as 'a lovely man who'd do anything for anybody', or 'kindness Itself'. He spent his free time conspicuously working for others, which earned praise and gave legitimate scope for being nosey. He was legendary for offering his own and his family's services as labourers and dogsbodies to friends, neighbours, the vicar or any passing stranger who seemed in need of them, which they usually weren't.

He was featured in the local free paper every few weeks, broom in hand, leading a residents' clean-up campaign or frowning at a chassis-busting hole in the road or some similar matter he was protesting about. In the latest photograph he was pointing to a sycamore twice the height of nearby houses. He and his supporters were demanding it be saved for posterity while the occupants of the terrace were pleading with the council to fell it before it fell on them.

'When you've done the staves,' he continued, 'get the wheelbarrow and bring the rest of that gravel to me and Harry.'

Lowering her arm Erica suppressed the desire to hit him, to lunge at him, tear out what was left of his hair. Some day, she promised herself. Some day. She dropped the stinking carcase in her bucket, shinning to the ground as fast as her numb body allowed. Unzipping her overalls she tugged them off with determined haste.

'I can't. I have to go now.'

'Go?' His brow corrugated, 'don't be stupid, man. Go where?'

'Remember Mum? You said I was to give her a hand. You said you're too busy to take her today.'

They glared at each other, the rising sun making glints in his spectacles, turning the bristles of his moustache to copper wires. Erica tossed her red curls and his face soured. For the first time she saw she no longer had to tilt her head to meet his gaze. In case he thought it was fear and not the weather making her teeth chatter she gritted them firmly, threw the overalls in the carrier of her bike. Without waiting for permission she took her jacket, shrugged it on.

8

'Oh, this is very nice,' he shouted, fists on hips. 'Wonderful. You're going to let everyone down again, are you? It's what we've come to expect from you. How am I supposed to get the job finished when one of my men is skiving off on the least excuse?'

Erica folded her arms, 'and how is she supposed to get the weekend shopping on her own? You know she can't.'

His gooseberry eyes sparked, 'watch it, lad! Don't use that tone with me! I've taken note of your insubordination lately.'

She knew he was in a ferment over this project. For years Ned Soames, the decrepit churchwarden, a retired gardener who kept the grounds like Chelsea Flower Show, was the vicar's favourite and an obstacle in Alb's path. As his assistant, Alb was in a role he despised, but found impossible to relinquish because of the kudos. Then came a miracle. In the same week the vicar retired, Ned went to bed after watching his favourite 'Carry On' film, and never woke up. The new vicar, Mr Coulson, was a blank sheet on which Alb was trying to write himself large.

Turning her back Erica clicked on bike lamps, swung her leg across the saddle. She was about to make for the gates when he clamped her shoulder, tightly bunching the neck of her jacket so she was unable to move.

'Wait.'

'What?' Her voice was muffled. She tried not to show how difficult he was making it for her to breathe.

He wagged a finger in her face, 'very well. I'll let you go. But only because she needs watching. You're responsible if she doesn't stick to my List, y'hear?'

'Right.' He let go and she jerked away from him then remembered, 'Dad, we need the key to the freezer.' He was silent. 'To put the fish fingers and stuff away,' she prompted.

He frowned. 'No, I'll open it when I come home at twelve. Take the cool bag.'

Her lips compressed as he stamped off with hunched

shoulders. He loped to the back of the hall where Harriet, her other sister, was mixing concrete. She saw him inspect it then take the spade and jab at the grey mound himself.

Her feet were so devoid of sensation it made cycling hard, then hurt more when the circulation throbbed back with waspish force. Increasing speed she bowled painfully through Riffton Hackets, the faded Manchester suburb where they lived. Although only three miles from the city centre it had an odd air of worn-out gentility. Pairs of crumbling stone gateposts leaning towards each other and pointless decoration on buildings made it more reminiscent of a country town than the scene of periodic shootings, bank raids, drug swoops, and the occasional police helicopter hovering at midnight. The district had grown around the eighteenth century Hackets Farm, long vanished, but there were still open spaces, remnants of woodland, a water park. A century ago it had been nicknamed 'the debtor's retreat' but over the years its pseudo-rural character had gained a certain cachet. Along with what passed for the normal population it was a preferred location of media types working for the television companies in town, plus artists, writers, college lecturers, the odd rock musician and the standard quota of urban crazies.

Apart from a milk float and a purple jogger the streets were nearly deserted so early on Saturday. Most people were sunk in the bliss of pillows, sleeping off last night's hangovers and related excesses. Passing rows of Victorian villas Erica was envious to see closed curtains. The indulgence of extra sleep was never granted in the Wakes household, not even on holiday. At Polperro last year the alarm clock was set for six, as it was at home. Her father said, 'I've paid good money for the time here and I'll not have you waste any by lying unconscious.' It was her sisters who paid for the cottage hire but that was a minor detail. Alb ruled them all, and each month they handed over three quarters of their wages for him to dispose of as he saw fit.

A wool hat couldn't prevent the wind biting Erica's ears

10

almost to amputation. To block the pain she transformed the ride home with thoughts of Gareth. Was it really only days since she'd been on the first date of her life? Actually been kissed by a living, breathing guy? One kiss. All through the morning's toil it had been like a pocket heater, a small, glowing memory to ward off the bitter weather and Alb's nagging. Being called 'fool', 'oaf', and 'waste of space' hadn't got to her as badly as usual. It failed to ignite the smouldering anger that was her defence against him. That date had changed everything, dispelling her deepest fear. Now she knew she was not, after all, as loony as the rest of her family. With luck she wouldn't turn out like her sisters.

She tried a daydream. A lie-in with Gareth. Oh yes, that would really be something. Heaven in spades, with him chief angel. She conjured up a luxurious bedroom. Crimson walls, a fire crackling in the hearth. He was twining long, muscular limbs round her as they writhed, naked, on silk sheets. She hadn't yet seen him without his clothes but her imagination filled the blanks.

Unfortunately, the thought of bare flesh chilled her to the bone. She shivered. Swiftly the phantom bed was covered with a duvet having the highest-ever tog rating. Over it she tossed a wolfskin rug, decided that was environmentally unsound and cancelled it, substituting a blanket crocheted in the Andes from alpaca fleece. She considered hot water bottles. No, not unless Calvin Klein had started doing them.

For a finishing touch she added a throw designed exclusively for her by Donatella Versace, hand beaded with crystals in a motif of wings. She and Gareth would be so hot, so amazingly, boilingly hot as they made love under the covers, as they licked each other's sweat, nipped and sniffed and pressed each other's crevices, it would seem that their hair was melting, the way Clare described it as being when she did it with her Darrel.

'We groan like monsters, like whales in their death throes,' Clare had said. 'We can't help ourselves.'

The two girls had been together since nursery school and were at the same sixth form college. Once they were into their teens and Clare became a beauty who always wore the latest fashions, Erica developed a gnawing conviction that her friend would·dump her. Clare had other mates so why should she bother with someone rarely able to invite her home, who had no clothes, no money? Erica even lagged behind in discussions of television as her family's viewing was censored, all the popular soaps having been progressively axed from Alb's approved list.

Clare was her lifeline into the ordinary world. Oh, for a normal life like Clare's. Your parents divorced and both remarried. Treats heaped on you to assuage their guilt. Clare and her sister lived with their mother and stepfather, visiting their affluent father and his wife at weekends. Everyone got on and Erica observed that being able to divide yourself between households meant people had more space and didn't get on each other's nerves so much.

Most of the girls she and Clare went through school with dated boys from their final year in juniors, or so they said. The others said they didn't bother with men on principle and it was uncool to judge your worth by some bloke's opinion. It was enough to be your own woman. Erica knew she wanted to agree but it would be a lie. Sure, she wanted to be her own woman, but with her own man. She knew it wasn't politically correct to even think it, and as the birthdays ticked by to a boyfriendless seventeen she spiralled into despair.

She felt it shaming to lead an existence more restricted than that of most fourteen year olds. It was doubly frustrating to live in a city that partied at the least excuse and feel you weren't on the guest list. The problem was a matter of time as much as of money. Of course the pubs and nightclubs, the mega-star pop concerts, were beyond her means. But because weekends were spent in unpaid toil for her father it left no space for all the free fun on offer. Manchester existed in a state of ongoing celebration.

Public entertainments were staged all year round, not only by the council, but one or other of the diverse ethnic groups in the city. Hardly a week passed that there wasn't some sort of festival, parade, dancing in the streets, candle-lit rally, music, fireworks. When she could get away she went with Clare to these events, which reverberated in her mind during the dreary hours at home.

Having grown up with her father constantly telling her she was rubbish, Erica knew the antidote was to find a man who would assure her otherwise. She had a recurring nightmare. Night after night she dreamt she wore a transparent designer outfit, her breasts uncovered as she dangled by the neck from a hanger in a wardrobe, gagging for air, unable to move. The door was locked so nobody could see the gorgeous dress showing the swell of her hips. She was kicking her feet, opening her mouth in soundless cries. Trapped.

Until Gareth happened. When Erica told her about him, Clare was so pleased she loaned her Nichole Farhi trouser suit and the boots she'd got at Christmas, for her friend to wear on the date. It seemed Clare could even guarantee he wasn't a mad axeman or crackhead as her cousin knew him from a footballing connection.

Erica first saw him in Riffton library. She'd actually noticed him every Saturday for weeks, but in the way she noticed things in shop windows, desirable but out of reach. With such rock star looks she guessed he was bound to have some smart city babe in tow. Then one day the two of them happened to be working on adjacent computers. She couldn't resist taking sideways peeks, examining more closely his even features, his row of silver earrings and nose stud. She took visual sips of him. She drank in the way his straight hair was highlighted on top, the sides cropped shorter, chevrons shaved in. His combats looked new, expensive, and a huge, padded leather jacket hung on the back of his chair. In my dreams, she told herself. He turned his blue glance on her and she flushed, concentrating on the screen.

Having finished her assignment she went to a favourite bookshelf and was leafing through *Gourmet Dinners For The Millennium* when a hand came over her shoulder, pointing to Oyster Prawns.

'I've done that one. Have you tried it?'

She looked at him, astonished. His deep voice made her pelvis feel like it was being softly hoovered. It was impossible. This god couldn't be chatting her up.

She said, 'there isn't room for me to cook at home.' She couldn't very well say she wasn't allowed to. 'I borrow recipe books because I like looking at the photos.' It sounded stupid.

'Same here. They're my bedtime read. Better than detective novels. I do try things out a lot. I've had disasters, like putting in a tablespoon instead of a teaspoon of ginger one time. Had everyone yelling for water, but I'm improving. Now I'm on a catering course, at City College.'

She nearly gasped out loud. A catering student! Sex and cuisine, the two things she thought about most, those twin icons of redemption that seemed so unattainable, were materializing in front of her. Embodied in this fantastic person.

They checked their books out at the desk then stood under the library's classical portico. Discussing how to grill glazed chops and the best way to prevent mayonnaise curdling.

'Do you fancy seeing a film tonight?' he asked.

It was like being given a sheaf of tenners then having it snatched away. Of course she had only been kidding herself, basking in the pleasure of talking to him. She had to refuse, explaining, in a lighthearted manner, 'I would but it's my parents. They can be a right pain. They're old-fashioned like you wouldn't believe. I practically have to have a pass to get out of the front door.'

But he persisted. Surely there was one night? Erica remembered Alb's next Neighbourhood Watch meeting was in another street. She could use that old standby, 'tea at Clare's so we can do homework together.'

'Wednesday. Yes, Wednesday. But I'd need to be back by half-ten.'

'No problem. We'll go to the early performance and have time for a coffee afterwards.'

Wednesday evening started well. Although the multiplex cinema was not the most romantic of venues, Gareth held her hand during the tense bits of the film. His fingers were still curled round hers as they came out and headed for the burger bar in Piccadilly. Instead of going down the busy main road they cut through alleys behind the backs of office buildings. Their pace slowed. They looked at each other and both visibly held their breath. They stopped by a parked car and he leaned towards her.

Then that kiss. She felt the strong cushion of flesh push against her mouth and wanted it to go on and on. The tip of his tongue ran very gently along her parted lips. She'd read up a lot on tongues in Clare's teen magazines, from which she'd gleaned most of her knowledge. She thought of a Reader's Letter that described it as 'a slimy slug crawling past my teeth,' and braced herself. But, surprisingly, he hadn't put it inside her mouth, just brushed backwards and forwards. She was unprepared for the running rill of pleasure that rose between her legs, sent a quiver up her spine. She hadn't expected the dizzying sensation of sinking into the pavement. Of falling in love.

They stood that way for several minutes. Gareth's lids were closed, then he recollected himself. He put an arm round her shoulders and they walked on, not speaking. There was a feeling of something tremendous happening. As they came into Piccadilly Square the lights of the hotels and the passing traffic floated them along. The spell broke when they bumped into two noisy college mates of his who, oblivious to meaningful looks from Gareth, invited themselves to Burger King and talked non-stop about people Erica didn't know. She felt gauche, out of it again.

They stayed until there was only time for him to see her to the bus, filling up at its stand.

'Sorry about that. Will you be in the library, Saturday?'

'Yes. I think so.' She was leaning round the luggage shelf as other passengers squeezed past.

'My Gran will be in Leeds for the day. I've a key to her place. If you can get away that afternoon - ?'

The bus was pulling out, the folding doors closing. She nodded at him, giving the thumbs up.

As she passed the shops on the main road it was getting lighter. They were still closed apart from the newsagents which had a solitary customer. Her face was turned to an ice mask by the rush of air and she worried about her lips drying. She was desperate to reach the Vaseline before they cracked, making them useless for the purpose she had in mind for them later on.

She pushed the pedals faster, anticipating what might happen this afternoon at Gareth's Gran's house with a mixture of dread and excitement. No crossing your bridges, she warned herself. Wait and see what happens. Of course she'd be careful. Oh God. Was she supposed to organise condoms? Was he? Did they come into the agenda? She hoped they didn't. She hoped they did. She couldn't afford them anyway. It was too soon, she hardly knew him. But she wanted him. If she didn't do it he'd lose interest. If she did he'd think her a slag. In spite of their longstanding friendship she'd feel a fool asking Clare at what point you did it. She felt tears rising and her heart thumped as she turned on to Wellburn Park, an estate of Thirties semis slumbering behind their gates. Veering left she whizzed into Turvey Close, narrowly missing the paper boy, who fell in a hedge yelling, 'Stupid Cow!' With a screech of rubber she halted in the driveway of Number Nine.

16

'Hello, love. You've got rosy cheeks.' Doris Wakes paused from apple peeling as Erica swirled into the kitchen.

'It's perishing out. Feel, Mum.' She laid the back of her wrist against her mother's cheek, sending a sympathetic shudder through the slight frame. Doris put down her knife, switched the kettle on.

'You're going to eat another breakfast before we leave.'

'Better not. He'd find out. Just give me a hot drink.'

But Doris busied herself getting out the frying pan, lighting the gas. From the fridge she took an enamel plate on which was an egg, a rasher of bacon and half a tomato.

'Oh, Mum, I can't. That's your allowance,' Erica protested but her stomach signalled, 'empty.'

'I didn't fancy it when we got up and I don't now. I've had toast. Besides, I've not been working outside like you. How's it coming on?'

'How is it ever. We're being slave-driven into the ground, tested to destruction so he can prove to Mr Coulson What A Friend He Has In Albert.'

'Erica!' Doris made a fishmouth of disapproval, 'what would he say if he heard?'

'Well he can't.' Erica bent her knees and slid up against the radiator, running her arms across it in a swimming motion to get warm. After a minute she went to soap her chapped hands under the hot tap and unscrewed the Vaseline jar. Patting them dry she gingerly smeared on soothing gunk.

'You shouldn't criticize him like that, love. People rely on Dad. Folk come up to me and say they don't know what they'd do without him.' Doris's pale eyes pleaded for agreement.

'They'd manage, that's what. I keep telling you, he invents things to make them think they need him. Honestly, Mum, I've said before, if he must play the ministering angel why not do it for real? Assist on a soup run in town? We wouldn't mind helping with that. But this lot - ' She gave a snort, 'how many of them have new cars each year?'

'He's very sincere about helping the local community. He is, you know. He says to me it's about nurturing our district, Doris. Don't run him down, love.'

Erica felt the familiar mixture of irritation and pity her mother roused. Did she really believe that bullshit? Probably. She seemed to believe everything he told her. As she herself had grown Doris seemed to have shrunk, protruding ears and straight hair accentuating her mouselike appearance. Erica lifted the lid of a pan that simmered on the cooker, sniffed, frowned.

'Not stew again, Mum. I wish you'd try something different. I've got dozens of recipes you could do, within his price, using his permitted ingredients. It'd make a nice surprise.' She had scrapbooks full of notes and clippings, cook books from the Oxfam shop, magazine articles Clare saved for her.

'Change his Saturday favourite? I couldn't. Besides, it's just the thing for a March day.'

Erica went to her shoulder bag hanging in the hall, rummaged in the pockets and found screws of paper. She glanced at one and put it back, remembering a strange evening of smoking at her friend's, wondering if she would give it another go. The others she took into the kitchen.

'Clare's stepmother dries her own herbs. We'll zest it up.'

'Don't. He won't like - '

But Erica had tucked bay leaves between the potatoes and sprinkled sage on top. Taking the ketchup bottle she shook it into the pan.

'There. Not much, but an improvement. He didn't notice the last time I added tomato sauce and it tasted better, didn't it?'

She longed to prepare something simple but tasty in this kitchen, stuffed mushrooms, an authentic paella or even a decent lasagne. The cooking was stuck in the l950s because her father insisted on Doris dishing up things he'd had as a boy: Grandma's sludge casseroles, suet puddings to cement your entrails. The family regularly sat down to offerings from a wartime recipe book Alb's mother had given him and Doris on their first wedding anniversary. He liked the sheer economy of it. Potato added to eke out flour, carrots instead of sugar, miniscule amounts of meat. Not for ecological reasons; he just hated to spend money.

Doris lifted Erica's breakfast on to a plate and set it before her with a mug of coffee. She kept glancing at the stew. Erica patted the top of her head.

'Mum, it'll be fine. When I'm a famous chef and open my own exclusive eaterie you'll know I was right. However he rants he can't force me to stick with computers after next year. But for now we'll let him think he can, eh?' She knew her mother wouldn't betray this confidence to her father for fear of the consequent eruption.

Half an hour later, kitted with rucksacks and bags, the two women got off the bus at the huge supermarket in Hulme. Weak spring sunshine had removed the chill, making the day more cheerful. Doris's habitually subdued spirits lifted as the doors slid open. The place was magic to her.

She came here once a week, always with Alb who didn't allow her to shop without him, except for bread from the local precinct and fruit and veg, for which she was allotted a certain sum. At the beginning of their marriage, when she was about the age Erica was now, he'd told her, in a kindly way, it was wiser if he decided what groceries they bought. He was better at managing things than she was. And then, they agreed, as she wasn't very good at figures it was less for her to have to worry about.

Supermarkets exuded a glamour that, to her puzzlement, people hardly noticed. It was such an outing to go trawling with Alb up and down bright aisles as music played in the background. To browse through troves of glittering merchandise made her tingle with enjoyment. She delighted in choosing a jar here, a tin there, even if they must be ones he approved. She liked to immerse herself in the sheer brightness of the place, the shapes, the colours of bottles, packets, the silver names on chocolate boxes, cheeses, crusty new loaves, the amber glow from batteries of cooking oils. And today she'd have the rare satisfaction of being a proper customer, the person who actually paid at the checkout.

Now, with only her daughter for company she relaxed. Erica didn't make her feel stupid, letting her take as long as she needed to locate things on the List. This must never be deviated from. Each Friday night Alb made it out after his bath. He wrote the List in a notebook balanced on his dressing gowned knee as Doris sat at his feet, clipping his toenails into a Marks and Spencers bag. He would carefully check the prices of everything from the previous week, comparing till receipts, noting any increases. He had a strict rule that as they went round the shelves each item bought must be crossed off.

Doris dawdled contentedly through her purchases. She picked up a jar of mango chutney, admired its label, replaced it.

'Get it if you want, Mum. I've some cash from Harriet.'

'It's all right.' Doris took a jar of sweet pickle instead, crossed it off.

Erica sighed. As well as pushing the trolley she carried a wire basket containing illicit shopping not to be seen by her father, some sweets, make-up, a magazine. She didn't receive pocket money. Her pleas to be allowed to take a part time job, like other girls her age, were derided by her father. When she wasn't studying, he said, he'd find plenty for her to do helping him. He was the one to provide for her needs. You've no bloody idea what they are, she'd thought. He was unaware her sisters, and sometimes Clare, gave her money. Accepting it she burned with angry gratitude, hating her position of charity case.

As she passed the cosmetics shelves she put a packet of tampons in the basket. With a quick glance round Doris hid it under the magazine.

'Mum,' Erica was exasperated by such prudery, 'you make me feel like a shoplifter. He isn't here, you know. He won't see them.'

But Doris was unable to prevent a flush to her cheeks. Although it was unthinkable such things would ever appear on the List she was unsettled by the sight of them. They were always bought from the chemists with money her older daughters gave for such expenses. Yet it felt like her husband was there, his face creasing with distaste at what he only referred to obliquely throughout their marriage as 'female matters', and then only in connection with herself. Never her girls. On the television at home sat an egg-timer so that the set could be switched off during the commercials, in case one of them showed such unmentionables, or anything else that might offend him, then switched on again when the three minutes of sand ran out.

Erica said, 'look, these have to be seen at the checkout. If it bothers you I'll take them through first.'

'Mrs Wakes. Doris, my dear.' They turned to find a permed woman grimacing through wrinkled lipstick.

'Hello, Mrs Copeland. How are you?' Inwardly Doris shrank. The Chairwoman of The Friends Of St. Chad's always had that effect on her.

'Bravely soldiering on. Ruled by my allergies. Did I mention I've developed another? Newspapers. I'm a victim of printers' ink. I was innocently reading one day when, without warning, The Guardian exploded my bust in a rash like the Milky Way.' She unbuttoned her jacket, then the cardigan beneath before they could demur. She leaned forward, pulling clothes away from herself, inviting them to peer down a dark, Damart well. 'See? In a swathe across my chest. Doesn't that remind you of a sheet of suppurating bubblewrap?' Doris frowned politely and Mrs Copeland re-fastened herself. 'I'm just back from a little cruise Donald arranged to raise my spirits. But enough of my suffering. How are you keeping? And Erica, dear, how are you?'

'Okay.' Erica moved away to collect a packet of cereal then continued along the aisle, putting distance between them.

'At that age, isn't she?' sneered Mrs Copeland understandingly.

'She's a good girl.' Doris was defensive.

'Oh, they all are. I drove past the hall on my way here and Albert was hard at work with your other two. Such amazing public spirit. I'd never have persuaded my Sarah to do anything like that, once she was grown up. She was too careful of her looks, too busy courting. But then yours aren't interested in that sort of thing, are they? Let's see, what age are they now? Nineteen or twenty?'

Doris hesitated, not wanting to admit it, 'Harriet's twenty two. Bernadine will be twenty four in April.'

A bunch of gnarled twigs, weighted with rings, grasped her arm.

'I'm glad I met you, dear. I wanted to speak about the flowers for tomorrow'.

'Didn't you get the bucket of narcissi I sent?'

'Yes, thank you. Albert brought them. We're arranging this afternoon but I'll need more tulips, a lot more. The frost's causing havoc. They're so wonderfully showy but such a price in the florists. Albert said you'd help.'

'Oh?' Doris stiffened.

'He said you've several tubs. Would you oblige, d'you think, my dear? About six bunches.'

'Scrounging old tart!' shouted the secret voice that lived in Doris's skull. 'Go on,' it urged, 'tell her. "No. Piss off, Missis!" '

She heard herself reply, 'I'll bring them when I come to do the cleaning after lunch.'

She thought regretfully of the bulbs she'd planted last autumn, now unfurling crisp blooms under the kitchen window. Maybe she could transplant something else to admire as she worked at the sink. She chided herself with being uncharitable in wondering why Mrs Copeland didn't bring some from her own, well stocked, acre.

'You should've stood up to her,' scolded the voice. 'What a wimp.'

'Sustenance! Fuel for the workers!' Alb's shout to Doris was jovial as he strode in the back door, followed by Harriet and Bernardine. They took off their shoes on newspaper laid ready in the scullery and washed their hands. The girls wearily took their places at the table but Bernardine got up as he ordered her to check the van, parked in the street, was locked.

'She's in her stockinged feet. I'll do it,' said Erica.

'Is your name Bernard? Get on with slicing that bread.'

He selected a key from his belt fob and called for the List. Doris brought it and opened the cool bag on the counter top, laying the contents out in neat rows. He unlocked the chest freezer and checked off each pack of frozen food before handing it to her to put away.

'We'll need a chicken to use tomorrow and the sausages for Monday,' said Doris.

He peered at her over his glasses, 'sausages? Did I specify them?'

'Oh yes, Alb. See, here's your menu list for next week.' She handed him a separate sheet of paper, watching his face as he frowned over it.

'Hm.' He took a chicken from the freezer. 'You don't need sausages till Monday morning. You can ask me then.' He put the lid down, locked it, and began to go through the dry groceries. Most of them had been put away when he stopped and held up the jar of sweet pickle, staring as if it were an alien artifact. In a reasonable voice he asked, 'Dor, what d'you call this?'

Her hand flew to her mouth. She went pale. 'Oh no. I thought it was - oh, I'm sorry, Alb. How could I be so stupid?'

'Own brand, you see, Dor. It's their own brand made up

with a similar label. Clever stuff. But if there's one thing I will have it's my proper Branston, the genuine article. When a man's slogged at his job all week, strained every muscle, to keep his family, he deserves the pickle of his choice, not an inferior substitute. Don't you agree, Dor?'

He folded his arms, watching her with a penetrating stare. Her face crumpled.

'I'm so sorry. I'll take it back on Monday.'

His smile was tinged with sorrow, 'and spend more bus fare? I don't think so. Never mind, love. It's only another of your little mistakes. We've coped with them before so I'm sure we can overlook it this time.'

Near to tears, Doris went to fetch the lunch. Erica wondered what shape the wound would be if you stabbed someone with a breadknife. She brought over the plate of bread, her mother followed with the reheated stew, now transferred to a tureen patterned with frogs and missing a lid, an heirloom from an ancestor of Alb's. When everyone was seated there was a pause, then, clasping his hands, he bowed his head. Erica's spoon clattered to the floor. Slowly he raised his eyes and she contorted herself to retrieve it from under the table and regain her chair.

'For all these many benefits we are grateful, O Lord,' he intoned. They all 'Amen'-ed the word 'benefits' making Erica think of beige envelopes and Child Benefit which, to her irritation, her mother still received for her.

'Pass your plates, men.' Alb brandished the ladle and began serving them, leaving his own share till last and, as a matter of course, awarding himself the largest portion.

When Erica was a child she thought all fathers were the same. In every house there had to be a bad-tempered man who bossed people round and told them all the things they couldn't do, couldn't have. Someone who must be deferred to at all times. She grew up in a household where it was accepted that nobody must ever contradict her father, but now she saw the craziness of their domestic set up, the injustice tolerated by the rest of the family.

There was a reason why he ruled unchallenged by any of them. Erica watched Doris and thought of that frightening time a few years back. What it was like to come in from school and find her mother gone, leaving a silent husk of herself in the armchair; unmoving, unresponsive. Staring into space in the same position she was in when Erica left that morning. Her father's disapproval of her mother's illness became a miasma permeating the house. Angrily ashamed, he didn't want the neighbours to know.

'This won't do. You must pull yourself together, Dor,' he kept repeating to the dumb figure. 'It's disgusting, lads having to do housework while their mother sits around,' he said later, when between them the girls were keeping things going. But he didn't offer to help in any way.

Erica, then aged twelve, took it on herself to face his wrath, pulling aside the cloak of secrecy to call the doctor. He recommended Doris should be admitted to a psychiatric ward for treatment. Alb wouldn't hear of it, fending him off with a very convincing performance. The doctor left believing Alb was a veritable Florence Nightingale, the concerned head of a strong family who would take care of Doris at home. In fact he kept away from his wife, avoiding all contact as if she had a disease that might transmit to him.

Erica recalled the hours she spent massaging her mother's neck, hands, feet, leading her around. Talking to her, coaxing her to eat, making sure she took her medication, until, after more than a year, Doris returned to a fragile semblance of herself. She was stronger now but it didn't take much to upset the balance. Sometimes, when Erica argued with Alb, Doris would shake. 'Look what you've done to your mother,' was his triumphant shout. Doris was his most effective curb against any insurrection.

There was silence except for the scrape of cutlery until Doris's quiet voice, trying to sound steady, volunteered, 'people were looking over Number Seven this morning, Alb, the same ones as before. It's said, 'Sale Agreed' on that estate agent's board such a long while I suppose they're the new owners.'

'Hmm.' He was put out at not having been there to spot them first. He glanced through the kitchen window towards next door, invisible behind its thick hedge. 'What were they like?'

'Two young men, very smartly dressed. With ties.' she added. Alb looked suspicious.

'We'd go a long way to get neighbours as nice as poor Mrs Trevis.' He shook his head, a sentimental droop to his moustache. 'It's a true saying, Dor, they don't make 'em like that any more.'

'It was a shame she died,' ventured Harriet. 'She was such a dear gran to us.'

'No, Harry, she was a friend. You've got a Grandmother. My Mother, Mrs Wakes, is your Grandmother. Express yourself properly, man.'

Harriet bent her ginger head over the food. She thought fondly of Mrs Trevis who had given her that first Barbie on her sixth birthday. Dolls were forbidden so it was amazing the way their neighbour persuaded her father, in her cut-glass tones, that the child, ill with measles, must keep the gift. Alb was awed by the fact that, in her youth, Mrs Trevis was on the staff of Buckingham Palace, had spoken to members of the Royal Family and was then, with the same mouth and vocal chords, speaking to him. He tended to cave in when anyone outside his family asserted themselves to him. So the old lady had her way. A precedent having been set, each subsequent year Harriet received another doll. Once grown up she continued to buy her own, mainly from boot sales.

Good old Mrs T., she kicked off my collection, thought Harriet, happily picturing her half of the room upstairs, lined up to the ceiling on two sides with Barbies, and similar teendolls, another hundred in drawers under the bed.

'Until we're quite sure it's sold,' said Alb, 'I'll continue to check the place for tidiness. It's nearly spring and an overgrown garden would let down the Close. Can't look at it today, of course. This afternoon I'm finishing the fence with Bernard while Rick and Harry smooth off the path.'

'I won't be able to, Dad,' said Erica. 'Em, I've a load of homework.'

He stopped eating, a potato poised on his fork, 'do that later, or tomorrow afternoon.'

'The library won't be open then and I've booked time on a computer. I did remind you.'

'Of course! Oh, of course! This is more important than St. Chad's, isn't it? This is more pressing than God's work.'

'Er, no, Dad. But you do keep saying you want me to do well in Computer Studies. There's a queue waiting to use the library ones. I need to grab them while I have the chance. With me not having my own -' deliberately she trailed off, assuming a regretful expression. She ignored the thoughtful look she got from Bernardine.

'I'm not made of money. Of course I'd buy something for your education if I could afford it,' he growled. 'Your own computer! Huh! I didn't have so much as a calculator at your age. Did I say calculator?' He gave a bitter laugh. 'We had to reckon by using our times tables.' As ever, his reasoning was quite illogical. 'Go on then. Sneak away and leave us in the lurch. Bear in mind the inconvenience you've caused me.'

'Sorry, Dad.' She tried to look it but images of Gareth, waiting at the library, got in the way.

Alb continued chewing then gave a bellow, 'Ugh! What's this?' He picked a dark object out of his teeth. 'What're you thinking of, woman, it's a privet leaf in the stew!' He prodded the plate, 'and another!'

'I, er -,' Doris looked confused.

'They're quite harmless,' Erica intervened, 'they're bay leaves, you know, for giving extra flavour. And it's not Mum's fault. I put them in.'

He got to his feet, rushed to the scullery with his plate and scraped it into the trash bin.

'I knew it tasted funny,' he snapped. 'Halfwit! You've made me waste food, you interfering fool. How many times must you be told, lad? Keep your nose out of the cooking! The cooking is what your mother does. Dor, make me a cheese sandwich.'

Later, after the others had gone, with Alb's shout of, 'back to work, men,' and she was washing up with her mother, Erica thought of *Poisonous Plants*, a book owned by Bernardine, who was in horticulture. She spent a pleasant few minutes fantasizing about the effect of a ground up laburnum seed in her father's next meal.

CHAPTER TWO

Doris brought tulips from the garden and laid them, wrapped in damp newspaper, in the carrier of her bike with a bag of cleaning things. Fastening her coat she turned to Erica.

'Bye, love. Don't work too hard.'

'See you later, Mum.'

Erica went upstairs to embellish herself with the inadequate materials to hand. Lingering in the shower she let it sluice the morning's frustrations down the drain but was annoyed to find she was staring at the wall tiles. Again. Stop it, she told herself. How symmetrical, how perfectly matched they were. Stop it. Each time she saw them it brought back the traumatic weekend last autumn she'd spent tiling the bathroom. Three times her father had made her re-do that row. She'd had to whip them off before the adhesive dried, scrape them clean, start again. Cutting the ones to fit round the basin and lavatory was a nightmare. Score and crack. Score and split. Alb standing in the doorway, grimly supervising, both of them aware he was willing her to make mistakes. She tried harder, got worse.

'One stroke with the cutter, I said. One! There, you've done it again.' The more he criticised the more her errors multiplied. By the time it was done to his grudging satisfaction she'd spoiled twenty tiles. Which he'd made her pay for from her savings; all her birthday money gone.

She concentrated hard, making the memory fade in the background and a hologram of Gareth step out of the wall and lather her all over. She rolled her head luxuriously as he caressed her wet hair, she felt his touch down her body. The sweet fancy came to a sudden halt as she realised the real thing was probably on his way to the library right now.

With the carefulness of long practice she blotted herself completely before stepping on the bathmat. No drop of water must sully the carpet. After removing all trace that a human had been there she went to her room. The use of talc being prohibited in the bathroom, on the grounds of dust pollution, everyone powdered by their beds. She unhooked a giant drawstring bag from the door, opened the neck and stepped in, pulling it over her shoulders. By feel alone she shook talc from the drum she held, spreading it over herself. On Alb's instructions Doris had sewn each family member one of these useful powder tidies which were regularly shaken out when the sheets were changed.

Erica wondered how she could dress alluringly from her pauper's wardrobe. She owned three pairs of overalls, one passed on from Alb, two pairs of jeans, T-shirts, a few sweaters from charity shops, and her college clothes that had lately served as school uniform. Her only dress, a gift from her grandmother for her to wear to church, was ankle length. She could at least have made it appear fashionable if it were black. But navy blue! It was like a warder's uniform in a Dickensian women's prison. She felt that to borrow something else from Clare so soon might overstrain friendship.

Adept at customizing her uniform away from home she considered hitching up the skirt waistband to show off her long legs. But the cold prohibited exposure so she pulled on jeans. Her college sweater really was awful, her only decent one in the wash. Picking up the one she'd taken off she put it to her nose. It stank of church hall, pigeon corpse, Alb's bullying.

Going into her sisters' bedroom she foraged in Bernardine's tallboy. They'd had a row the last time she found Erica trying on her clothes ('I don't want you to so much as touch them! Ever!') but this was an emergency. Erica went through the drawers, being careful to neatly re-fold the lacy underwear, the mouth-watering tops, some still in their shop carriers. She drew out a sweater, new and unworn like most of the things Bernardine was forever buying.

Bernardine dressed in thick outdoor clothes and walking

boots to the garden centre where she worked. At home she was constantly in the garden or greenhouse, when not labouring on one of their father's schemes, so she always wore the same garments. Besides, Erica knew, if her sister appeared in anything from her hoard she would be subjected to a sneering barrage from their father. His barbed comments, his 'what do you look like, man?', always made Bernie draw in her horns, curl back in her shell. He tried it with Erica too but his constant, 'get your hair cut, lad', only prompted her to cultivate her luxuriant red mane to below her shoulders.

Erica slipped into the silky garment. The mirror confirmed its speedwell hue matched her eyes. She knew it looked better on her than on Bernardine's chunky figure. Of course Bernie would sulk a bit when she found out but then she should help her younger sister at this crucial point. Things this yummy were wasted on a person who just got them for the sake of ownership, who had no interest in anything but plants. Secure in the knowledge her family were at a safe distance, Erica applied makeup in the way Clare recommended and hurried to the library.

Gareth had his back to her as she came in. Seeing him at a computer sent a surge of animation through her. She stood nearby and slid a book out, dropped it deliberately. He looked up. She'd explained that the librarian knew the Wakes. A cautious check showed she was listening to details of a reader's piles operation whilst making sure the cassettes were in place on the talking book he'd borrowed. Erica hadn't actually ordered computer time so she browsed the shelves until Gareth finished. He came and stood by her.

'My bike's out front, chained to the railing,' he murmured.

'So's mine.' He handed her a folded sheet of paper, a photocopied page from the A - Z. She started to giggle, 'James Bond, OO7.'

'The address is marked. Follow me along Princess

Parkway but give me a head start. Although Gran's out till late her street's full of old curtain twitchers.'

He left and she followed a few minutes later, managing to keep him in sight all the way through heavy traffic to Platt Fields park, then trailed him up a maze of terraced streets that faced on to it. He turned into a back alley. She got off and wheeled her bike as he went through a gate, which he left ajar. She was about to follow when a woman came out of the next one. Erica continued to the end of the alley then, as the neighbour disappeared in the other direction, returned, and saw Gareth waiting to put the bikes in the yard and usher her indoors.

An iron range dominated one end of the living room, a guard protecting embers in the grate. Taking the poker he stirred them to life so the flame reflections on the walls reminded her of the bedroom she'd conjured. She blushed, glad of the dark afternoon.

'Give me your coat.' It was the first time she'd felt his touch since their date. He eased the sleeves down her arms, put both of their coats on a chair, shooed a cat off the battered couch, shovelled coal on the fire. He fiddled with the radio until he found the right music. Erica heard her heart beating.

'Cup of coffee. Or tea?'

'Er, coffee, thanks.'

She watched him fill the kettle then put it down. In a rush he came over, took her hand, pulled her down beside him on the couch. The moment of truth. What did she do next? Play it by ear. By mouth. He was kissing her. At first a tentative bussing which became more urgent. In the gloom she saw his lids droop, his eyes take on a faraway expression. His arms went round her and he sighed. A sigh. What did that mean? He was stroking her back, her jeaned hip. Erica stiffened. She didn't mean to pull away but found herself sitting up straight. There was a pause as they moved apart.

'I'm glad you're here, Erica.'

'Me too.' She should have talked to Clare more about the etiquette of it, so to speak.

'Other girls I've met aren't interested in the things I like to do.'

What was that? He did mean the cooking? She edged away slightly. Not ropes and stuff, surely. Was the fact he had a few piercings significant, she wondered. A recent programme on S and M she and Clare watched had them both shuddering, looking away. Was it just some people or was everyone into it? A guy as smart looking as Gareth would do what was cool. Wondering which other parts of him were punctured made her nervous.

He leaned over, pulling something from under the sofa. A whip? Maybe manacles? A bottle of wine? She mustn't let him get her drunk. The Readers' Letters page always warned about that. He lifted a pile of books on to his knee. *French Country Cooking, Delia Smith's Winter Collection, Fifty Ways With Eggs.*

'I thought we'd look through them together. I want to point out ones I've done. Then, if you like we can, well, only if you fancy it, cook something.'

'Great.' A whoosh of relief. 'Yes. I'd like to, but, I did mention I hardly know how.'

'French onion soup is good for beginners.'

French onions. Show me your French onions. It sounded sexy. Did he mean what he said or was it an erotic code she was ignorant of?

But he was wrapping her in an apron. They stood together at the worktop, slicing onions, her eyes watering, mascara smudged, as he explained about using a bit of the onion skin to colour the soup. Of course it was a relief he hadn't grabbed her as soon as they were through the door. She'd never intended to let him, had she?

'This is ready. Can you get the bowls from the dresser? I brought some of my homemade bread to have with this. Russian black bread. Ever tried it?'

She shook her head and as he ladled soup her anxiety

faded. She felt calm, happy. Yes, she did want him to proceed slowly. He turned on a lamp, infusing the room with a sexy cosiness as they sat down, exchanged smiles, took up spoons. Aah, Erica thought, this is how the beginning of love should feel. This is right.

An ominous metallic sound came from the hall. A front door key.

Leaping up, they stared at each other. With amazing speed he removed one of the soup bowls, emptied it back in the pan, grabbed her coat and bundled her into the yard.

'There'll be a fuss if she finds you here. I'll distract her while you escape.'

'But, shall I meet you later?'

'I have to stay and talk to her for a while, give a reason why I'm here. See you at the Whitworth in half an hour?'

Disgruntled at finding herself ejected into the darkening afternoon she pulled on gloves and cycled to the art gallery where she hung around, staring unseeingly at exhibits. She sat in a side room where large windows reflected in glossed woodblock. It was empty but for six vast paintings, herself and a ragged bundle laid, snoring, across two seats. None of the attendants were aware of him, or perhaps had noticed and were letting him be. Maybe he's intentional, a piece of installation art, Erica quipped grumpily to herself. She imagined venting her frustration on the tramp, rolling him on the floor. Getting a punch on the nose.

It was a lot longer than half an hour before Gareth joined her.

'I had to stay and have the soup with Gran, pretend I'd made it for when she got back from Leeds or she'd have been suspicious. Her mate threw a wobbler at the station so the trip was cancelled.' He gave her an apologetic squeeze and she relented. 'Not that she wouldn't make you welcome but I'll have to introduce you to her properly or she'll nag my old man about it, cause hassle for us. You know what they're like.'

'Yes. Only too well.'

They wandered round the Whitworth holding hands but it was useless being surrounded by other people. She felt his lips on her cheek as they contemplated a Chinese textile then he bought her a coffee in the restaurant. She declined his offer of its renowned chocolate cake, tried not to salivate as he ate his. She was horribly aware she had only one pound twenty pence in her pocket and couldn't bear to be beholden yet again. It was dark as they rode back to Riffton, parting, at her request, at the top of Wellburn Park.

'Will I see you next Wednesday?'

'I don't know. If Dad's meeting isn't at our house. Honestly, Gareth, he's like nobody you ever met. On another planet.'

'Is it always this bad when you're seeing someone, having to hide it?'

Erica felt a fool and bit her lip. Oh, go on. Tell him.

'Well, I've never actually gone out with a guy before.' She'd blown it.

'No kidding?' She saw his eyes light up.

Next instant she was enveloped in the warmth of their body scents, his jacket lagging her against the cold.

'You do want to see me again, Erica?'

She nodded.

'Can I ring you?'

'No. If he answers the phone he'll go ballistic. Let me see what's happening and contact you.'

Doris finished vacuuming the last stretch of maroon runner along the church aisle then put away the Hoover. She set to with cloths and beeswax, polishing the pews as Mrs Copeland's group sorted flowers on a trestle by the altar. Normally there would be a wedding in progress but, unusual for March, none was booked today. There'd been a funeral earlier in the week. After the service the deceased dear had departed via the crematorium so, as was the custom, the floral tributes were sent back to be recycled as church decorations.

Doris went closer to admire the arrangers' work. They were building displays on brass stands polished by herself the day before. One woman was doing a bowl of spring flowers, pushing their stems into Oasis. She made a clumsy movement, knocking some of the tulips Doris had brought earlier to the floor. Doris retrieved them for her, attempting to stick them back.

'No, my dear. If you don't mind - ,' Mrs Copeland's talon pushed her firmly aside. 'It takes training to be a flower arranger. Everyone here has done a course. So, though I know you're trying to help we'd rather you didn't touch anything.'

Mumbling an apology Doris moved away under patronizing stares. She decided to work near the back of the church, retreating to where they couldn't see her.

Alb had volunteered her as ecclesiastical drudge when they first came to the district. 'It's a privilege for you to clean God's house, Dor. It's what's called a practical prayer. You know, you've got the example of me praying that way all the time.'

She hadn't minded. Now it was as much a part of her routine as being an onlooker at the supermarket. When she was there alone she liked being in the beautiful building which had the feel of a cosy, old-fashioned parlour with its stained glass and cross stitch kneelers, wall hangings and mahogany.

The latch of the side door gave an echoing rattle and Alb came in to be greeted by the flower arrangers.

'Albert, hello.'

'Good afternoon, Mr Wakes. What do you think?'

'Good afternoon, ladies.' His tone was gallant. He paused to admire their handiwork, 'those are magnificent.'

'We do our best.'

He circled a stand, wearing his awestruck expression and there was the flirtatious flutter he anticipated. They beamed on him.

'The skill. The way you've got that professional finish. You're talented enough to make a living at it. On television.'

Doris, watched from behind a pillar as they played their game. A chill came over her. She never got used to the way Alb's tone to other people was so different to the one he used at home, the charming manner he switched into with strangers.

He spotted her and came over. Lowering his voice he said, 'I'm borrowing the extension cable from the vestry. Bernard was too stupid to put mine in the van.' He watched her polishing for a moment, bent to straighten a kneeler that was out of true. 'See you at supper then,' he said, walking away.

Watching him stride down the aisle revived a memory of the first time she saw him. Carrying planks into Firbank Grange where he was one of the carpenters working on an extension. She learned he had been in the army. A corporal, and this was his first job since returning to civilian life. Her instructions were to keep the workers supplied with beverages but she did so with lowered glance, too shy to say much. But Alb began to chat to her, seek her out, so the other men teased them.

She was flustered, unable to believe anyone was interested in her, certainly not this tall, sandy haired man with his attitude of authority. She knew nothing of men, having been brought up in a children's home run by Anglican nuns. The sexes were segregated so she rarely saw boys except at church.

School was a trial. The main lesson she learned was that she was completely stupid because the sisters told her so. They also said that as God made her that way, if she always remembered to be humble, she would be acceptable to Him. There were two things she could do well, looking after the younger children and housework. The convent used the girls as domestic staff and she got in plenty of practice dusting, washing, scrubbing the ancient flagged floors. By example, and severe beatings where they thought it necessary, the nuns taught her to be quiet, respectful and handy at taking care of their own needs. Ironing their clothes, fetching water for baths, emptying their chamber pots. When she left the home at sixteen it was a natural progression for Doris to go into service. She was found a live-in position by a nun whose cousin had four children.

Dipping her cloth in the fudgey beeswax she spread it on a pew. The honeyed, clean scent transported her to the panelled hall of Firbank Grange. She'd liked it there, been fond of the children. It was such luxury to have her own room in the attic. Food and lodging were part of the wage but it was wonderful to receive a small amount of money each month, which her employer insisted she put in a savings account. Every so often she took Doris to town to choose shoes and clothes. Doris would have preferred going on her own as Mrs Kay always overrode, in the nicest way, what she wanted to buy. She was there almost two years when the alterations to the house began, bringing Alb.

'That's a pleasant young man,' Mrs. Kay said. 'Steady. He's very taken with you, and the age gap isn't so great.'

Doris wasn't sure if he attracted her. She didn't know how romantic attraction was supposed to feel. Rather she was in awe of him, the way he could charm people, and flattered he should bother with her. When he asked her out she went because everyone expected it. She shuddered, thinking of that day in Chester. She'd never been in a restaurant before and was convinced everyone was watching. They'd had fish and chips and the peas were so hard they rolled off the fork, bouncing to the floor. She cringed red-faced apologies to Alb. His smile was indulgent, almost satisfied. He told her not to worry.

But she found Alb very worrying. He was always asking her what she'd like to do then telling her what it was. He took her to meet his mother whom she found terrifying. Tall and gaunt like her son she could have been the twin of

Sister Agatha, the head nun at school, and shared the same knack of pinpointing peoples' shortcomings.

A few months after they'd met Alb said, 'I've decided to marry you, Dor. That's what you want, isn't it?'

'I..I don't know.' She was seized with fright.

'Yes. You do, Dor.' Firmly he gripped both her hands so she couldn't move, towering over her. His stare held her in thrall.

'It's - too soon. No thank you, Alb.' From somewhere she mustered the courage to refuse.

'The end of September will be a good time. That's a while yet.'

'I don't think I will, thank you all the same,' she said politely, trembling with fear.

He squeezed her hands harder. 'We'll have to see about that. Because you're young you don't know your own mind, Dor. We'll help you make it up.'

He released her abruptly and she watched him march away, that 'we' ringing uneasily in her ears. She tried sticking to her resolve but Mr and Mrs Kay got to work on her. Summoned to their drawing room she faced stern looks.

'Doris, we hadn't thought you the kind of girl to lead on a man for the sport of it,' said Mr Kay gravely.

'Me? Oh, but I never -,' she stammered.

'It's not nice, dear,' Mrs Kay reproved. 'You don't want the reputation of being a tease, now, do you?'

'Oh no, but I didn't - ,'

'Poor Albert is very upset that you're playing with his affections. He's told us you've promised to marry him but refuse to name the day. That's foolish, my dear. He's a man who'll take care of you. You need that.'

'It's a sound offer. You'll not get a better.' Mr Kay's frown was judgemental as he regarded her thin figure.

After several more weeks of her resistance being worn down on all sides, Doris found she was the reluctant Mrs Wakes.

Massaging the shiny wood she wished she could rub away the past. She sat back in the pew, recalling the start of their married life, in a tiny terraced not far from Alb's mother's house. Having lived in the country all her life Doris found the city daunting. But Alb helped by managing their finances, doing the shopping, which became his lifelong habit, and selecting the furniture and fittings for their home, after consulting his mother.

That first year Doris worked hard to adjust, doing everything she hoped would please him. He told her he understood how strange it was for her not to have set rules after being used to them at the convent and with her employers. Just to help her, so she knew where she was, he drew up lists of his requirements and showed how he expected things to be done. The first time she saw him angry was when he complained about a bill and she suggested she could get a job to help the budget. He rounded on her.

'You're mine and I keep you. If a man can't afford a wife he shouldn't have one.'

'But it's the Seventies, Alb. Lots of women go out to work.' She'd been bolder then. More hopeful.

'I'm the breadwinner. Understood?' Something in her expression made him relent. 'You'll have enough to do when my sons arrive, Dor.' He gave her an encouraging pat. 'You'll be proud to raise them in the home I make. This place is a beginning but someday I'll buy us a house we'll make into a real little palace.'

Doris looked up at the painted cherubs on a window. Brian had been born at the end of that year. She was allowed to see him briefly before he was rushed to the neo-natal unit. And away for ever.

The condemnation in the faces of Alb and her mother-in-law when they visited was scalding. It seemed to take them forever to walk down the ward, between rows of beds, each with a cot beside it apart from hers. Alb looked outraged, embarrassed, deeply ashamed, as he pecked her cheek. His mother sat, clutching a handbag like a vulture its prey, regarding her with contempt.

'It happens to a lot of women. You'll get over it when you have more.' It was a command. You didn't argue with Lily Wakes. After a tense twenty minutes she said, 'we must go, Albert. We mustn't miss our bus.'

The next pregnancy filled Doris with dread but Alb was hopeful. Terence clung to life for a week. After that they didn't talk about it. The house became ever more perfect as Doris sewed and Alb did ambitious joinery, admired by the neighbours. They began to ask his advice and when he went round to show them how it was done, he'd decide he could do it better. He also volunteered Doris to do people favours. Basking in local approval he unbent slightly. But, apart from a brief kiss as he left for work, for a long time he didn't touch her.

Then at Christmas Alb forgot himself enough to get merry at a neighbour's social gathering. In bed later, he rolled towards Doris, pulling her into his arms. They didn't make plans this time. He almost ignored her condition, told her it was best kept to themselves as long as possible. Yet on the night of her labour he stayed beside her at the hospital. Before going to the waiting area he whispered, 'this time he'll be all right, Dor. You'll see.' Afterwards he stared, dumbfounded, at the baby in her cot. 'A girl. I can't believe it. You've had a girl,' he accused.

His disappointment was palpable. The way she'd let him down was a stultifying ache behind her ribs. She was with him when he tried registering the child as Bernard Wakes. She wanted to stop him. She wanted to scream. She thought she was going to be sick. It was the scandalized clerk in the registrar's office who pressured him into adding an 'ine' to the name.

He showed her the true depth of her inadequacy when people sent gifts; little bonnets, dresses printed with rosebuds. They went missing and she later found them wrapped in newspaper in the dustbin. He actually went out and bought plain Babygro suits.

'I don't want you dressing Bernard in anything cissy,' he said. 'Suitable clothing, Dor. Suitable clothing from now on.'

When familiar signs returned she was too busy caring for Bernardine to worry. Scans were not then commonplace and when Harriet appeared Alb looked grim.

Doris found it frightening that so much went unsaid, yet without actually stating it, Alb conveyed how she was to bring them up. She knew she must obey. Without him, she couldn't care for herself and the children. She'd never been on her own and despised herself for the way she needed other people to tell her what to do.

She realised it was a crazy way to live yet had no option but to play along. She trained herself never to refer to them as 'the girls' or 'she' to Alb. She got round it by calling them 'the children' or naming them, something in her sticking firmly to Bernardine and Harriet. To him they were Bernard and Harry, 'the lads', 'my men', terms he only used within the family. In public his speech and manner were tailored to his listeners.

Once the girls were on their feet he practised toughening them.

'You're not killed. Stop that blubbing, lad,' he'd say to a tumbled down child, shaken with sobs. On walks he never slowed his pace, shouting at the stumbling little figures to keep up, and they ran, eager to please. It amazed Doris how soon they picked up on the family conspiracy, knowing they must not act as other girls did when with their father. The way teachers and other people behaved to them was not relevant.

He avoided touching them, either in punishment or play, hardly ever held their hands or picked them up, something for which Doris tried to compensate. The children even learned what toys it was all right to ask for, which ones were taboo. Bikes, sports gear, cap pistols. The boxes of tools brought a bonding of sorts when he taught them woodwork. As they got older he drove them relentlessly to do every labouring job, however dirty or dangerous, around the home or for the neighbours. But, in spite of his campaign to make them the boys he wanted, Bernardine remained a gentle soul who loved growing things, and Harriet, courtesy of Mrs Trevis, partially slipped through his net, being canny enough to keep the teendolls in the confines of her room, a private passion he ignored.

The family's move to Wellburn Park with its streets of little palaces came when Alb found a better job. Doris was dismayed at another pregnancy, the possibility of more failure. It wasn't discussed but when a friend said, 'I suppose you want a boy this time,' Alb looked affronted.

Red faced, red haired, with the scrawny ugliness of a newly hatched parrot, Erica roared into their lives. Her first word was a rebellious, 'no!' yelled at her father. Of course she didn't stand a chance and also fell under his dominance. But where her sisters obeyed in the useless hope of gaining approval Erica did it resentfully, because she had no choice. Doris's admiration for her youngest daughter went deep. Erica was the person she'd like to be if she had the courage.

She was shaken from her reverie as the door clashed again. A woman came in with a holdall and spoke to Mrs Copeland. They glanced in Doris's direction. Spotting her behind the pillar they beckoned and she joined them to receive ingratiating smiles.

'Doris, do see what Julia has brought us,' Mrs Copeland lifted a large, tarnished copper pot from the bag.

'Lovely, isn't it?' said the other. 'It was left me by an old uncle but it's sat in the garage ever since. 'When Susan said she needed a large container for tulips I remembered it.'

'You've got your metal polish and rags. Would you mind, dear?' Mrs Copeland handed Doris the heavy object.

'I'm afraid I just didn't have time,' said the other woman.

43

'I must dash. Taking the girls to their skating.'

They went off, chatting, and Doris sat on the steps of the pulpit, working Solvol over the dull surface of the pot. She rubbed as hard as she could but the metal shone patchily first time round. She went over it again until she achieved a pinkish gleam. She was pleased and rolled it on its rim to the women.

'It's come up nicely. The blooms will look well in it, Mrs Copeland.'

'Yes. It's a handsome piece.' She examined it, 'but look, dear. There are unsightly dark patches. Would you see what you can do?'

It was like being back at school. Doris remembered the nun who taught needlework. She often made Doris stay in through playtime, unpicking a hem she hadn't sewn straight enough. She scrubbed away at the discoloured patches without result.

'I'm afraid they won't come out.'

'Vinegar might do it,' suggested one of the others. 'If you put dirty copper coins in it they clean up.'

'That's worth a try. Would you mind getting some from that little shop across the road?' Mrs Copeland put a fifty pence piece into Doris's hand.

'Tell the shrivelled prune to do it herself!' commanded the voice in Doris's head. The voice often visited her at such times. Or if she was feeling low she called it up and it responded. She'd given it a name, Casey. When she was ill that time Alb said, 'you're a head case, Dor. You're so hopeless I don't know what we'll do with you.' Casey urged her to tell Mrs Copeland what she thought. But the words were ghosts that would not become real, could not escape. Doris put her coat on again and went out. Alb waved from his concreting but she gave a brief nod and hurried by. A big, icy bubble was expanding in her, constricting her breathing.

When she returned she heard the women in the church hall next door, gossiping over a tinkle of teacups. They were talking about the new vicar. She heard her name mentioned.

' - and Alb is a sweetie, giving so much help. A pity his wife's a clinging ivy. I've heard he has to do everything for her, poor man.'

Doris rubbed the vinegar fiercely on the spots and they disappeared. Someone made a remark and there was a gale of laughter. She collected her cleaning things and fled without saying goodbye. As her daughter had done earlier she pedalled home vigorously, arriving breathless. Where Erica had been elated her mother felt ready to snap in two.

She went into the immaculate front room and, still in her coat, stared out at the Close. The young couple from opposite were unloading groceries from their car. The Asian family from further up strolled past with their children, chatting. She was seized by a feeling she often got, that she owned nothing, not even herself. Distractedly she saw a man pasting the word SOLD over the sign in next door's garden. A fresh lot of people for Alb to charm. She wondered what he would ask her to do for them.

'Go on,' whispered Casey, 'there's only one thing you want. You know what makes you feel better.' Doris hurried upstairs and went into her elder daughters' room. Placing a chair by Harriet's built-in wardrobe she climbed up, took a suitcase from one of the top cupboards. She'd told Harriet it was full of household papers and receipts, knowing she wouldn't bother with it. It was a safe hiding place from Alb who never set foot in the girls' bedrooms, which he regarded as abominations he had to endure on his premises. To him there seemed a strange force field which prevented him stepping over their thresholds.

Doris opened the case and quickly lifted out a stack of *Gossy* magazines. Seated on the floor, her back against the bed, she began to read through the current issue with burning urgency. Alb had expressly banned all women's magazines, other than *The People's Friend*, which never featured the word 'orgasm' on its cover. Doris derived a fearful but satisfying thrill when she fiddled the vegetable money every Friday in order to buy *Gossy*.

The bleak, diminished feeling was still there but began to subside as she read the true-life stories she relished. It was comforting to know other peoples' traumas were far more horrendous than hers. Her problems were small compared to the experiences of these women. 'I Thought He Was My Grandad But He Was Really My Brother', 'Jilted At The Altar For A Mud Wrestler', 'Look What Plastic Surgery Did To My Body', 'In Love With My Mother's Twin', 'People Say I'm Quasimodo', 'His Rodent Obsession Broke Us Up'.

Doris sat, elbows on knees, absorbed in the chaos of other lives. Yes, she was lucky. Alb would never leave her for a forty stone stripper or keep mice and rats in the freezer to feed a collection of birds of prey. How awful it must be to come home from the factory and find your husband in bed with the milkman, like this poor woman who stared out at the reader with downturned mouth.

After reading her fill Doris flicked back to the beginning and, taking a biro from Harriet's table, worked her way through her favourite features. The competitions.

Sleuthwords. It was a type of crossword where you joined one word to another, then took letters from certain coloured squares to make the name of a well-known television personality. That was difficult because of her restricted viewing but she always managed to get it by deduction.

She turned to another and another, 'Win a weekend for two in Torquay', 'Win a Fiesta car', 'Win a new kitchen'. She filled in the answers strip on the back page, put it in an envelope, stamped and addressed it. Of course she never won anything but that didn't matter. It was something she could do. She got the solutions right. Feeling quite calm again she put the envelope in her pocket, for posting later, returned the suitcase and went downstairs.

CHAPTER THREE

Hurry up. For God's sake hurry it up! Erica thought, itchy with irritation as the congregation plodded towards the end of the final hymn. To prevent herself dying of boredom she'd spent the service having sexy thoughts about a carved angel who looked a lot like Gareth. There was a whole row of them along the roof beams, each playing a musical instrument. Hers had a lute and she imagined him as a medieval pop star. Pursued by maidens in ye kirtles chucking their knickers on ye stage. No, they didn't wear them in the middle ages. So what did they? Nothing? She couldn't imagine that. Messy.

Harriet was also contemplating the angel with the lute. That tunic he wore was pathetic, the sleeves badly cut and baggy. A crap shade of red too. What he needed to wear was a big collar, ancient Egyptian style, on a jacket tapering to the waist, to define the figure. Something like the outfit she'd recently made one of her Kens. She only owned eleven Kens, which she realised was a bit disproportionate to the three hundred and twelve teendolls. But the fun was in designing costumes for her girls, as she thought of them.

Harriet often mentally dressed those around her in more interesting style. She'd amused herself throughout the sermon by putting the vicar in a lilac satin jacket and sarong skirt with silver platforms. And old Mrs Lee, sucking peppermints in her pew, was unaware her sensible wool coat was now black-fringed leather with studs down the front and 'Beelzebub Chapter' on the back.

Harriet glanced sideways at Bernardine, one of her favourite fantasy makeovers. She did occasionally throw suggestions to her sister about her appearance, receiving the stock answer, 'leave me alone. Mind your own business'. It was immaterial to Harriet that her skinny self was drab as a sparrow. The way she looked didn't bother her because her enjoyment was in creating images for others, be they plastic or flesh. She was busily draping Bernardine in green velvet and feathers when the hymn came to an end.

At a signal from Doris her three daughters followed her through a side door into the hall. The large urn bubbled in the kitchen as they set out cups and filled plates with biscuits. They could hear the blessing, then the organ playing as those members of the congregation not staying on shuffled out. The rest flowed into the hall on a wave of chatter and queued at the hatch where Erica and Harriet were serving.

From her position at the counter Doris watched her husband. He entered wearing his social expression and chatting to the vicar, who was being verbally caressed at the centre of a little group. He, in return was massaging egos by telling everyone how lucky he was to have such supportive workers in his parish.

At first there had been doubts regarding the suitability of the new incumbent of St. Chad's. It appeared he began his working life as a Butlin's Redcoat before training as an actor. After appearing in repertory he'd toured in a rock musical, danced in a bread commercial and, amongst other jobs, had been an extra in *Coronation Street* before being called to the ministry. But the parish was won over by his charm. A meaty man in his late thirties, his pale hair and eyelashes gave him the appearance of an amiable storybook pig, eager to please.

He was a head shorter than Alb who was gazing down at him, with a look of ownership. 'Call me Jeff,' Mr Coulson had instructed his parishioners. His predecessor had not allowed such liberties and was always addressed as 'Mr Kerr' or 'Reverend'. Now, having leave to use the vicar's Christian name made Alb feel his own position was elevated. As Harriet passed him a cup of tea, the vicar leaned through the hatch to smile at the women.

'We mustn't forget what a part these ladies play in keeping things going. You wonderful girls, out in all weathers. And you do sterling work cleaning the church,

Doris. It always sparkles.'

'Yes. I keep my little group running on oiled wheels,' said Alb.

'Dear Doris is one of my team,' corrected Mrs Copeland at his elbow.

Driving home Alb informed them that Jeff Coulson (the words tasted good to him) liked his ideas for the grounds. He outlined plans for a giant rockery. The girls felt their spirits sink, knowing who would heave around any giant rocks. As they turned into Turvey Close they saw the sports car outside Number Seven but nobody remarked on the two young men who stood talking in the doorway until Alb spoke.

'Ah, what have we here?'

'The new owners, I think,' Doris told him. 'The ones I mentioned.'

'I'll have a word as soon as I park.' Alb was eager but first there was a set ritual to putting away the van on Sundays.

The three young women leapt out of the back, slamming it shut. Doris jumped out of the passenger seat. Harriet and Erica rushed to open the gates to the car port, Bernardine sprinted through to push up the garage door. They came back onto the path, standing like a guard of honour as Alb drove in while Doris went through the front door and opened the back to admit him. He hurried out in time to see the strangers drive off.

'You were too slow,' he growled, stamping upstairs to change his suit.

After lunch Erica sat in her room wearing ear plugs. Homework was an excuse for not being with the rest of the family but she was gratingly aware of her parents downstairs. It was her father's day to play his Country and

Western CDs. Although he practised stringency in household expenditure Alb knew it would have been false economy not to buy himself the latest, most luxurious sound system on the market. Curiously he also retained a radiogram in a wooden cabinet, passed on by his mother, on which he played his hoard of vinyl records.

The penetratingly mournful voice of Jim Reeves was a syrup seeping through Erica's floorboards to the ceiling and running down her bedroom walls. She wished she had a Walkman to drown it. She was gritting her teeth as she surveyed the greyness of the day. Pleading the cause of mutual study at Clare's was no good. Her father insisted they must all be together on Sundays so everyone managed to be on the premises whilst keeping their distance from each other. She wanted to ring Gareth but couldn't do it from home. There'd be a scene. Alb always minutely examined the itemised bill. She paced up and down her boxroom, feeling claustrophobic.

The doorbell went. For a crazy second she thought Gareth had come to see her. Then she heard her father welcoming someone, his tone cordial as he ushered the visitor in. Next minute Harriet thundered down the stairs. Ann. Erica wrinkled her nose at the thought of Harriet's friend. Ann, whose father was a city councillor, was one of the few people approved by Alb, because of her connections. She was a fragile hypochondriac of thirty whose graveyard complexion and protruding eyes put Erica in mind of Gollum, from *Lord Of The Rings*. She and Harriet were mutually obsessed with showbusiness and belonged to three fan clubs at newsletter level. They didn't favour the sort of bands and singers Erica liked, their interest being stage musical extravaganzas and Barry Manilow.

The two women came upstairs giggling and went into the bedroom. A minute later a sullen Bernardine came out and Erica heard her escape to the garden. She crossed the landing and put her head round the door. Harriet and Ann sat on the bed in the glow of a table lamp, examining the contents of Ann's travelbag. Erica nodded a greeting to the guest and came in.

'Hello. How's it going?'

They hesitated for a moment, not sure if she was mocking them as she sometimes did. But then, with a hint of pride, Ann took out two tissue-shrouded figures.

'She was about to show me her wedding couple.' Harriet took one of the figures and Ann unwrapped the other to reveal bride and groom.

'Why is Ken dressed as Elvis?' asked Erica. They glared at her.

'He isn't. In Hollywood at the moment white wedding wear with embroidery is very fashionable for men. Look.' Ann took a copy of *Hello!* from the bag, flicked a page open.

'Oh. Sorry.' Erica retreated and slumped on Bernardine's bed.

The room was like the cabin of a ship, not an inch of space wasted. Her sisters had each built in their own beds with drawers underneath, cupboards and wardrobes, their two tallboys side by side facing the window. All Harriet's wall space was taken up by a fixture of rows of wooden niches, redolent of the saint-encrusted west front of a cathedral, but filled with dolls. A high, free standing bookcase with shelves both sides divided the room and screened the sisters from each other's sight. Erica riffled idly through Bernardine's books. *Diseases In Vegetables, Water Gardens, Rare English Orchids*. She was quite surprised to see a dozen or so Mills and Boon romances tucked along the bottom shelf.

She was grinding her teeth again. She got up and went to the window. The long gardens of the Close backed on to those in the two streets either side and formed a wide area of trees and hedges. The sky had turned pewter and several houses had lights on or showed the blue flicker of televisions. She was struck by how lonely Bernardine looked in the middle of it, hunched over her monotonous chore of digging the potato patch.

'I will be true to you until the moon and the stars burn to cinders and the planets are no more,' chorused Harriet and Ann. They were reading a marriage pledge the model girlfriend of a footballer had written for their wedding. 'Deep as the deepest ocean, I feel my heart singing, I feel my thoughts flying -'

I feel my stomach heaving, thought Erica and went out. Leaving them to their Barbinalia she stole downstairs, her footfalls drowned by the cutesy tones of Dolly Parton singing *Applejack*. Grabbing her jacket she went out of the back door. Bernardine, absorbed in her task, was too far away to notice.

Erica edged her way along the hedge dividing Number Nine from what had been Mrs Trevis's. There was a narrow gap where it joined the back of the Wakes' garage and she squeezed through into next door's path. The hedge extended to the front, although there it was only waist high. Crouching to screen herself from the front windows of her own house she could see Alb bending to put on another CD, her mother knitting by the gas fire.

She sped to the phone box in the next street and dialled the number Gareth had given her. There was no reply. She was disconcerted, having rehearsed what she would say. She went for a short walk then tried again. It rang and rang. She knew he lived with his dad. Were was he then? She leaned against the window. He was out with someone. Worse, he was in with someone, in some girl's house. They were alone. Making soup. Making love. She swallowed, her eyes welling, and rang Clare.

'You just caught me,' Clare's tone was brisk, 'Darrel's here and we're going out.'

Erica immediately felt bleak. They were going out. Probably to visit at some cool flat, where people sat around smoking roll-ups, talked in an interesting way. Playing music that wasn't country and western. Maybe they'd take in a nightclub later.

'Where to?' she asked, her voice bright.

'The Irish Club. Darrel hadn't seen *Riverdance* before, can you credit that? I mean, what planet's he been on? But someone showed him a video and he's hooked. We're going to join this step class they've started on Sunday afternoons.'

Irish dancing was suddenly magnetically attractive. Erica longed to be banging her feet to a jig. She said, 'I only rang to ask your advice. About Gareth.'

'Oh?' Clare went into counselling mode. 'What's up?'

Erica described the previous afternoon. 'And now there's no answer. I'm kidding myself, Clare. I've fallen for him, big time. But I've this gut feeling he's out with someone else.'

'Yes, he is. A gang of other blokes. He's in a five-a-side against the White Lion today, with my cousin. You plonker! If he says he wants to hear from you, he does. Try tomorrow, before he goes out.'

'Thank you. Thanks.' She was laughing with relief.

As she returned to the Close she saw the sports car parked outside Number Seven and the house lit up. But her parents were still in their front room and she couldn't get in unseen. Doubled over she darted up the path of Number Seven as the side door opened and a man came out to empty rubbish in the bin. She was only feet away but he didn't look up.

'Have you found the frying pan yet?' he called over his shoulder.

'It's on the cooker, with an omelet I'm making you, in case you haven't noticed.' Beyond him she glimpsed the other man. Very tall with short hair. The door closed and she quickly dissolved back through the hedge into the Wakes' garden. Bernardine was coming up the path as she opened the scullery door.

'Taking a breath of air. Getting my brain working,' mumbled Erica, going in.

Bernardine didn't reply but followed and began unlacing her boots. She took them off, using an old knife to scrape mud from the soles. Erica wondered if she cared about anything that didn't involve soil. Then recalled the collection of paperback romances. From the front room came the voice of someone singing about their good ole houn' dawg who was gawn. She was halfway up the stairs when Alb came into the hall.

'Aren't you supposed to be working?'

'I am. I needed a drink of water.'

She went into her room and lay on the bed. She stared at the ceiling, her face muscles contracting upwards.

The sound of an engine woke Alb after midnight, sending him to the window. He noted a hire van parked in the drive of Number Seven, lights going on. Though the hedge slightly obscured his view, he was aware of figures unloading furniture into the house. He tingled with eagerness, wanting to join in, to rush round and tell them all they needed to know about the place. Supervise. Lend them ladders, screwdrivers.

He restrained the impulse. They might interpret his presence as a rebuke at having been disturbed. Reluctantly he went back to bed and lay awake a long time, anticipating the pleasure of interferences to come.

Next day was Monday but he was taking a half-day off, owed to him from the D.I.Y. chainstore where he worked. He waited until eight-thirty, which seemed about right for introductions, then carried an offering of tea and biscuits up the path. The tray prevented his knocking on the door but it already stood open. Good. They were up.

'Excuse me?' he called into the echoing hall. The dusty floor was dotted with cobs of underlay where the carpet had been pulled up, and some oriental rugs were flung over a chest at the end. He edged his way indoors.

'Hello there?' Cautiously he peered into the front room. Mrs Trevis's rose motif Wilton was still in situ, swamped under a chaos of furniture, fabrics and piled boxes. His gaze ranged with avid interest over a chaise-longue, a brass eagle lectern like the one at St. Chad's, and a huge purple pouffe in one corner. Then the pouffe shuddered, a pair of feet moved backwards out of it and he realised it was the posterior of a female.

'Ah. Er -' He retreated and the tray rattled.

'Eh? Is that you, luvvy?' Still kneeling, the woman turned to look at him from green eyes smudged with what was obviously yesterday's mascara.

'I'm Albert Wakes from next door. I wasn't sure if your gas had been reconnected.' He held out the tray.

'That's sweet of you but it has. I was digging out a box of mugs and thought you were one of the family come home from work. They do nights.' Her voice had a gravelled edge. Taking a cigarette from her mouth she showed a half moon of what was more than the standard amount of teeth.

'Put it down. As you've made it we may as well drink it.' He placed the tray on a low table and she grasped a chair to lever herself up.

'Allow me.' Extending a polite hand he found it engulfed in one considerably larger. As she leaned on him he had the sensation of an inexorable force pressing him down, reminding him of the time he was trodden on by a shire horse.

As she moved upward he was enveloped in overpowering colour and perfume. Like a genie from a bottle he saw her rise and expand into the robe she wore. And was aware of a corresponding shrinkage somewhere in his vitals as he gaped up at her. She was the biggest woman he had ever seen. At least six foot three and around eighteen stone. Her facial contours were slashed with expression lines under a bird's nest of grey locks springing from a gold scarf.

'Tundra Mae Tyler, darling. Pleased to know you.'

She parked herself on a chair, which creaked, and waved him to a cardboard box.

'Sit there. It's stuffed with books so it won't collapse under you. You be Mother. I have milk, no sugar.'

Obediently he poured from the china teapot he'd specially selected from the Wakes' display cabinet.

'I wasn't sure how many cups and saucers to bring.' He found he was stammering slightly, something he hadn't done since boyhood.

She took the tea from him. 'So, Albert, what sort of a place is the Close?'

'Oh, extremely nice. You find a very respectable class of person here. We're all supportive to each other. Very supportive. If you need help with anything, anything at all, you only have to ask me. Night or day.' He was in his stride now, on familiar ground.

'Do you live alone?'

The question felt like a criticism. 'Me and the wife have been married twenty-seven years,' he said defensively. He hesitated, choosing his words, 'There's five of us. Two grown up offspring. One in the teens.' What was he doing? He wanted to find out about her, not the other way round.

There was the juddering of a taxi outside. A slam. Someone came into the hall.

'That'll be my Germayn,' said Tundra. 'In here, luvvy,' she called.

A slender, red fingernailed hand came round the door and a young woman looked in on them. Alb felt his jaw drop. He had never seen anyone so glamorous in real life. She was something off the cover of a magazine. A sleek cap of dark hair swung against her pale skin, her lush mouth was a lipstick advert. She gave Alb an odd look.

As she came into the room he stared at her tall figure, wrapped in black velvet, the lycra gleam of long legs. She bent to kiss Tundra.

'Hi, Mumzo. Who's this?' Her voice was also husky, but lighter.

'Our neighbour, Albert, bearing gifts of Typhoo'.

His palms were sweating. He surreptitiously wiped a hand down his trousers and extended it to her. She had a surprisingly strong grip. He sensed something in her glance. Surely it wasn't amusement? He stroked the sparse fuzz on his head. It was like discovering someone famous living nearby. He'd often imagined what he'd say to Dolly Parton if they met. The thought of this amazing creature being close enough to make use of him in all sorts of ways turned him quite dizzy.

'Would you like a cup?' he asked in a reverential whisper.
'Thanks. Milk only.'

She took it from him, quickly gulped down the tea.

'How was last night?' asked Tundra.

'Pig of an audience,' Germayn yawned. Tell you later. I'm totally knackered'.

Unbuttoning her coat she flopped on to the chaise-longue, spreading her legs wide apart. In one graceful movement she whipped off her hair and frizbied it across the room. Stunned, Alb watched it fly through the air and land on the eagle. His mesmerized gaze took in the unmistakably male contours of the close-cropped skull. The high-cheeked planes of the face under its perfect makeup. Broad bones of wrists half hidden by bangles. Germayn's fringe of dark lashes closed.

'Must be going. Said I'd give the wife a hand with, er, yes... Must be off. Bye,' Alb, halfway down the hall, gabbled over his shoulder. As he shot through the gate he heard a burst of raucous laughter. It was only as he came into Number Nine he remembered he'd left the tea set behind.

'Are the new people friendly?' Doris glanced up from sorting the washing, then cringed, seeing his beetroot flush, the twisted glare.

'You have to show a few manners and that's what I was doing,' he ground out.

'Of course you were, Alb.' Unsure how to react she watched him drag out a chair and sit at the table, absorbing himself in the local paper. After a pause she asked. 'Er, what are they like?'

He took a deep breath, turned over two pages. Without raising his head he muttered, 'they aren't our sort, Dor. They don't look as if they're church goers. The less we have to do with them the better. Understood?'

CHAPTER FOUR

For the rest of that morning he was shaken. Pretending to himself he was not doing so he covertly watched Number Seven, difficult because of the hedge. He contrived some weeding in his weedless driveway so he could monitor Tundra as she moved objects about her front room. When old Mrs Trevis was alive he often saw her looking out, her shrivelled form occupying a small section of casement. Now the whole window frame appeared to have shrunk. The ceiling lamp was only inches above Tundra's head as she swayed to and fro, dominating the space.

Half an hour after his visit she returned the tea things. From where he skulked in the kitchen he heard her make the introduction, exchange pleasantries with Doris at their front door.

'It's nice to meet you, Mrs Tyler. I hope you'll be very happy. Mrs Trevis loved that house.' Doris gazed up in awe.

'Call me Tundra, darling. Yes, I'm sure we will. My boys and I suck the juice from life wherever we find ourselves.' Disgusting turn of phrase, thought Alb, but what you'd expect. 'Pop in and see us any time.'

'And if you need assistance do say.'

'That's kind, Doris. Your Albert's made the same offer so I'll let you know. Must go. I'm being inducted into my new job today. Bye.'

When she'd left he sprang forward, gripped Doris's arm, pulling her into the kitchen. She winced.

'Weren't you listening? Didn't you hear what I told you before?' She shrank against the wall. 'What d'you mean offering our help to those people?'

'But she said you already -'

'That was before I knew what they were like. No fraternising. Right?'

Her frown was puzzled. 'If you say so, Alb. It's just, she seems a friendly person. You were there such a short time

58

I can't imagine how they've upset you. And everyone knows you as such a good neighbour.'

'Is my wife trying to go against me now? Am I being criticized by my own wife?' His voice got louder. 'Do I or don't I know what's best for us, Doris?'

She gave a timid nod.

'I'm a vigilant man, Doris. Oh yes, I'm vigilant in protecting my family from -' he paused, 'the unpalatable. I'd prefer not to say it but you force me. In there I met one of the sons dressed in women's clothes. Women's clothes! And, for all we know, the other one may be the same!'

Grimly he waited for her response. She hesitated, wondering what reply to offer. At last she ventured, 'some fellows do, don't they, Alb? There's that United player that puts on skirts to match his girl's. And the comedian chap that wears lipstick and high heels. You know, the good looking boy who keeps reminding you he's a man. I believe he does book reviews too. Then I've seen a picture of Richard Branson dressed as a bride.'

Alb wondered if his ears had malfunctioned. His pupils dilated, he snarled, 'what're you saying? What've you been told about watching dirty programmes?'

'I didn't view any crossings-out, really I didn't, Alb. I stick faithfully to your highlighter. But they put trailers on for other programmes so often you can't help seeing bits of things.'

'Then switch off! Why d'you think we have the egg timer? I've said it before, I shall get rid of that television.'

'It'd be a shame though, Alb. Wouldn't you miss your gardening and travel, and the Country Music Show? I'm sorry. I'll be more careful.'

'You aren't guarding yourself against bad influences, are you, Doris?'

'I didn't watch any crossings-out,' she repeated. She was trembling, knowing what was about to happen as his expression glazed. He pushed her against the wall, held her by the collar.

'You're stupid, aren't you?'

Dumbly she nodded.

'I'd be failing in my duty if I didn't get you to improve, wouldn't I?'

'Yes.' It was a whisper.

'Down.' He slammed her to a kneeling position. 'Remind yourself of what happened to Lot's wife. She looked at things she wasn't supposed to.'

Doris stared at the floor, trying to imagine herself turned to a pillar of salt for watching news snippets.

'Pray,' he ordered, 'for God's forgiveness. And mine.'

She had learned from long practice to weep silently.

'Pray, I said.' He held her hair, forcing her head up.

She began to mumble the words and he released her. He stood, arms folded, frowning.

'My clean overalls weren't in the airing cupboard this morning. Where've you put them?'

She knew they were there but he was showing his displeasure.

'Shall I - shall I go and get them?'

'No. You'll stay there till I come down.'

He moved to the door and she glanced up. He pointed to the floor and she bowed her head again.

He bounded upstairs. As he changed in their bedroom he saw the sports car drive up. The man he supposed was Tundra's other son got out; smart in leather, bearded, carrying a long, black case. A musician. That was all the Close needed. Practising all hours. Bringing home other musicians, and it was well known what they were like.

Doris kept very still, the tiles cold under her bruised knees. Then she did pray, that she'd be lucky, that this would be the full extent of his outburst for today. Sometimes he broke things. Once, when he was annoyed with her, he'd walked over to the sideboard, jabbing his elbow at a vase, a wedding gift from the Kays.

'Oh. An accident,' he'd said as it crashed. 'Get it cleared up.'

Nowadays it was only her own possessions that were destroyed. When Harriet and Bernardine were children he often smashed their things. They learned early not to leave books or toys lying around. Once grown up they kept any valuables in the safety of their room. Curiously, he had only once trashed something of Erica's, when she was four. Irritated by her prattling to a teddy bear she brought to the table and was pretending to feed, he ripped it apart, tossing its limbs in the air. The towering rage of the pint sized figure matched his own, her rending screams vibrating through the house.

'I'm going to kill you!' She'd shrieked again and again, face contorted as she tried to rush at him, restrained by her mother. Even he looked taken aback, ordering Doris to get 'that mad boy' out of his sight. Ever after, a wariness, a state of armed truce, existed between him and their youngest. Doris was sure he suspected, as she did, that Erica was biding her time. One day she'd get him.

There was a time when he made them all kneel and pray before him for imagined misdemeanors. Now he only did it to Doris.

'Yes, you're a stupid woman, like he says,' Casey whispered to her. 'Stupid to let him push you round. You don't have to obey him. Get up. Go on.'

Doris knew the truth of it but was held in place by a force she found impossible to resist. She'd often been punished like that at the convent. When anyone shouted at her she couldn't help but obey. Disgusted with herself she drooped, helpless as she waited for him to release her.

Erica yawned, stretching to relieve the tension in her neck as she emerged from the Computing Centre on Oxford Road, which ran through the centre of the University campus. Her study group was coming out of a lecture on their possible futures in IT Yeah, she thought, yawning again, I do know how important it is to the world, the whole universe. And if I got to be a top practitioner it'd keep me in yogurt for the rest of my days. But I can't stomach the idea of spending my life as a project manager in front of a screen, that's all.

Having her own PC would be useful though, to download cuisine info. off the Net. At some point she'd get one, for the efficient running of her restaurant. She could have a database of her television appearances, all the articles written about her. 'IT is the lifeblood of today and tomorrow,' was a phrase their tutor used. True, thought Erica, but so is food. Unless the population itself is genetically modified good dinners will always be in demand. She'd create superb gastronomic experiences, arouse people's taste buds, make them lust after the fare with which she'd grace their palates. She saw an auditorium packed with her fans. Lights. Music. Everyone wearing an Erica Wakes badge, waving a fork and belching a song in praise of her.

The shadows were still white with frost but the sun made her narrow her eyes at its brightness. She jumped when it was blanked out by arms going round her.

'Gareth!' Her nostrils twitched with the scent of him.

'Clare rang last night to say you'd be here. I'm based down the road so I've come to take you to lunch.'

'I've got sandwiches.' She was still breathless with surprise. 'We could take them to the park.'

'You deserve better than a bench.'

In the nearby vegetarian café they chose a window seat, luxuriating in their mutual attraction. This time she wasn't awkward about him spending money on her. She saw that by allowing it she gave herself the pleasure of pleasing him.

'I tried to ring you this morning but it was engaged,' she said as the order arrived.

'My Dad on to a customer. He's a rep but he's changing to an office job soon. Which means -' he touched her hand, 'I'll have more chance to borrow his car.'

'Smart.' She thought of the two of them, out in the

country, miles from Alb. She took a critical taste of the food. 'Mm, not bad.'

Gareth forked some off her plate. 'Yes. Perhaps a bit heavy on the pepper. But they usually get it right. Try mine.'

She opened her mouth and he slid the morsel in.

'Gorgeous,' she mumbled, meaning him as well as the mushroom pie. And the day. And sitting here together.

Tapes of flute music played, imparting an atmosphere of sanctity to the place, its plain walls covered in posters for sweat lodge weekends, circle dance, barter groups. There were wind bells, crystals, mantra cards on sale in the shop part of it. And all the staff were becomingly thin, their slight bodies taking up their minimum share of space on the planet.

'What's so funny?' He echoed her grin.

'We're like the righteous ones, kind of biblical, y'know, not polluting ourselves with the flesh of beasts.'

'Or sinful additives. A temporary state for me I'm afraid. I'm doing spag bol for Dad and me tonight.'

'We've got pork sausages.'

'I do like veggie food but it can be taken too far. A vegan I knew wouldn't allow her cat to eat meat. Fed the poor thing on baked beans. The smell in her flat was terrible.'

The table shook. There were tears in their eyes.

'No hope for us,' Gareth giggled, 'a pair of ravening carnivores.' Lifting her hand he gently bit the fingers.

Oh, she thought. Oh. A shiver went up her back. The door of the wardrobe in her bad dream swung open.

Then he said, 'I've got Food and Beverage Management this avvy. Better make tracks.'

Unchaining bikes they rode together to his college, a curious Sixties folly popularly known as 'The Toast Rack'. They parted at the entrance, ungluing themselves from each other.

'Wednesday then?'

'Wednesday.'

Erica floated through the entrance to Keggs Dell College and encountered Clare, in paint spattered apron, in the wide corridor next to the hall.

'Art?'

'How did you guess?'

'Clare, you're a star. I just had lunch with him. Thanks.'

'Wait while I get coffee then tell all. Damn, the canteen's closed.'

She brought two Cokes from the vending machine to a row of tables along one side of the corridor where people worked or chatted. As they discussed Gareth and strategies to bypass the Alb problem, Erica was vaguely aware of doors at the far end opening and closing as students went through. Then something, a presence, prompted her to look up.

She saw a startling woman approach, walking with the ponderous tread of robed figures seen in state processions. Her flamboyant looks and great size were almost those of a carnival figure, ornately garbed, head and shoulders above the passing teenagers. A silver pendant swung from her like a sensor, long skirts swept the tops of turquoise boots. A couple of boys sniggered but were ignored. She had the unmistakable charisma that silences derision.

'Hi, Mrs Tyler.'

She paused to return Clare's greeting, looked with concentrated interest at Erica. 'Wonderful. Like a sunset. Nature or a clever bottle?'

Clare laughed, 'Erica's been my mate since we were five. She's always had that wild hair.'

'May I?' A large hand lifted Erica's tresses this way and that. 'Magnificent. We'll base something round her. Bring your ideas to the afternoon session, Clare.'

She gave them a benevolent smile and moved on.

'Who's that?' Erica goggled.

'The new art teacher. She starts next week but came in this morning to be introduced and shown the ropes before

Miss Dee scarpers with her bellyful of brat. Mrs Tyler kind of drew us in so we started to work with her there and then. She's staying the rest of the day. She's got this way of firing you up.'

'What did she mean, base something round me?'

'Relax. We won't chop it off. Probably take lots of photos of you and stick them over a model of your body. Yeah, I like that one.'

Erica went to the computer room, elated as she waited for her machine to boot up. The day's delight had been Gareth coming to see her but Mrs Tyler's appreciation of her hair, so despised by Alb, was an extra gift. She stared at the screen, thinking up an excuse to slip out to the phone that evening.

After college she usually cycled part of the way home with Clare, but tonight Clare and Darrel were catching the bus to a movie. When she went to get her bike from the shed Erica saw it had a flat. She suspected childish sabotage and watched everyone stream past, oblivious to her annoyance. Now she'd have to walk it, and fast. Her father would use this as another slagging off opportunity if she arrived late for dinner, and there'd be no chance of getting out. She remembered the garden centre where Bernardine worked was a quarter mile in the other direction, and Bernie had the puncture kit. She wheeled the bike towards the college gates as a battered estate car passed and stopped ahead of her.

'That looks sad. Where are you going?' Mrs Tyler had wound down her window.

'Riffton.'

The big woman got out and opened the hatchback, picked up the bike, swung it in with ease.

'I live there. I'll give you a lift.'

'Thanks very much.' They got in the car and turned on to the main road.

'Where in Riffton? I've just moved so don't know the place yet.'

'The Wellburn Estate. I'll say when we reach it.'

'That's where we are. You know Turvey Close?'

'I should! Our house is Number Nine.'

'I'm your new neighbour at Seven.' They stared at each other. 'I met your parents this morning. Your dad brought tea.'

'Yes. He'd be there the minute you arrived.' There was something in the girl's tone that caused her companion to give her a sidelong glance.

'Where have you moved from, Mrs Tyler?' Erica asked, not wanting to think about Alb.

'Oh, we've lived all over the place, but our last home was in Yorkshire. I ran a gallery in Hebden Bridge, as an outlet for the work of an artists' co-operative I belonged to. But, what with the paperwork and personality clashes it became rather idiotic. I spent more time sorting out disputes than doing my painting. Anyway, my sons and I have decided Manchester makes a better base for our activities.'

'Will you continue painting as well as teaching?'

'Ah, you see, Erica, teaching is the job I do. It buys time for painting. Painting is actually me.'

'That's exactly how I feel about cooking.'

For the rest of the journey her new neighbour listened as Erica outlined her ambition. It was like talking to an older version of Clare.

Bernardine unloaded stone hedgehogs from the trolley and arranged them between the flowering shrubs. There was a while to go before her day finished and each evening she found it more and more difficult to leave. She felt comfortable there. It was more her home than Turvey Close. Mr Gray, her elderly boss understood and appreciated her knowledge of plants, her willingness. Tasks were completed without anyone shouting at her, or acting as though she were a halfwit. And now there was Shaun, adding a new dimension to things.

Considering the size of the place it was remarkable the number of times she encountered him during the day. Land o' Green Nursery and Aquatic Centre covered several fields where most of the stock was grown in plastic tunnels for the outlet in the garden supermarket. This was a complex of indoor and outdoor areas, including a café, reptile house, gnome grotto and tropical fish cave. Anything connected with gardening was on sale. For every conceivable job there was a special tool, prodders, delvers, clippers, twisters. The merchandise ranged from heavy duty mowers through garden furniture, birdhouses, petfood, to a whole series of household items described as 'fragranced', destined for window ledges.

Shaun had joined the firm some weeks ago. When the boss brought him to where Bernardine was labelling fruit trees he smiled briefly, shook her hand, causing her shyness to well up. She rarely touched another person. She didn't risk letting people come close. Closeness meant being scrutinised, exposed. She tried to make some welcoming remark but it took a long time for her to get used to anyone new. This man seemed amiable enough and she supposed she'd learn to tolerate him as she did her other colleagues.

Although she was employed for her horticultural skills all the staff were expected to fill in for each other when necessary, especially in the shop at busy times, so she had to mix with people. She had acquired the knack of putting on a semblance of sociability. During breaks she joined the others in the staff area, but their talk was of lifestyles that didn't tally with her own.

Sue and Tina, the women who ran the shop were about her age, both single mothers. Their careful smartness increased her sense of lumpishness when she was in their company. They never knew how she imitated them. On occasions that she went into town she saw their kind of clothes in the shops. She only intended looking but always ended up buying. Taking her purchase from a rack she'd rush to pay for it and leave, never daring to try it in the dressing room. She reserved that for the privacy of her bedroom, when Harriet was out. For a long time she'd look into the mirror on the back of the door, then take the garment off and put it away.

Their conversation centred round their children, household problems and men. When they could get babysitters they went out together on what they called 'the pull'. They constantly comforted each other over some short lived relationship which had broken down. Sometimes they chatted to her with a touch of condescension and she would nod, put in the occasional quiet word, escape when she could. She knew they were nice to her because they classed her as a sad case.

With the recent improvement in the weather she resumed her habit of going to a favourite seat behind the greenhouses with her lunchpack to read a paperback in peace. She'd done that one unseasonably warm day last week and been disconcerted when Shaun came round the corner, hesitated as if to walk away, then turned back.

'D'you mind if I sit here?'

'No. There's plenty of space.'

He stayed at the far end of the bench and skimmed a newspaper. She put her book away. Her romantic reading was private, something she didn't want to be questioned on. He looked up then pointed out a piece in the paper about genetically modified crops and asked her opinion. They discussed plants in general, which ones were most popular with customers that year. Thankfully he didn't ask anything personal or venture information about himself the way most people did. In him she recognised her own reserve.

Where possible she preferred working on her own so she avoided him as much as she did the others. But the boss decided they were to co-operate on a project he'd designed. He wanted a spare piece of land turned into a feature that would encourage children to garden. Easy-to-grow plants, mini wheelbarrows, watering cans etc. would be sold, hopefully hooking a new set of customers. At one end there was to be a covered walk-in market stall, something well within Bernardine's carpentry skills. She was irritated when Mr Gray assigned Shaun to work with her but, as ever, didn't argue.

It wasn't anything Shaun did or said that annoyed but his presence unsettled her. He was as taciturn as herself, their exchanges prosaic. 'Is the plane over on your side?' 'Can you hold that end of the plank, please.' She just had a constant, uncomfortable awareness of him. Each time he glanced her way she became a mirror to herself, imagining how he was seeing her faults, the thickness of her body, the unattractive features. He complimented her on the way she did the job and she knew she was being silly. Of course he didn't notice her as a woman. They got along as fellow workers and were mates, after a fashion.

But in the washroom she sent questions to her reflection, resisting her lifelong avoidance of eye contact with the unpleasing image. A plain sort of face, she confirmed drearily. Grey eyes, largish mouth. A frizz of red-brown hair tied in a bun. Why should she care what he thought?

Of course she had imaginings around men, but only the ones she read about. They stayed safely between the book covers where she could join them, be whatever she wanted. There she was the feisty, gorgeous heroine they couldn't resist, that they strained to their manly chests, overcome with passion on the last few pages. Shaun was definitely not Mills and Boon hero material. Of medium height, his brown hair touched with grey, he was built with stocky strength, there were weather crinkles at the corners of his eyes. But whenever he listened intently to something she said, or his slow smile appeared, she wanted to look away. She created distance between herself and the others but he was so real it made her uncomfortably aware of the reality of herself. It dismayed her to find herself surreptitiously checking where he was all the time.

It was the day it was sleeting outdoors that the truth hit

her. Mr Gray set everyone to working under cover as much as possible. Although it was early afternoon, the dark made it a relief to have their break in the warmth of the canteen. Bernardine was there with some others when Shaun came in. He went to the counter for tea and the girl serving began to flirt with him. This set off Sue and Tina who had watched him walk across the room.

'Ooh, look out, Shaun. She'll have you for breakfast.'

He didn't respond but took the cup the girl passed him. She looked annoyed.

'Take no notice. They're always like that.'

'Come over here and we'll show you what we're like,' whooped Sue. She and Tina laughed.

He took a newspaper from his pocket and looked round for an empty table. He saw Bernardine but settled at the far end of the room. Undeterred, the two women picked up their cups and went to join him.

'Just teasing. You don't mind do you, love?' Sue plonked herself next to him.

He gave them a wry grin, returned to his paper. Tina leaned forward, pulling it away.

'Hey, c'mon, Shaun. You've been here weeks and we still don't know you. Tell us about yourself. Got a wife? Anyone?'

Bernardine was straining her ears. She glanced at him. He put up his hands in good humoured protest as Tina slid an arm round him. 'Come on, girls. Can't a bloke read the sports pages in peace?'

'A man of mystery!' The women made faces at each other. 'Playing hard to get. I like a challenge.'

Bernardine stood up. On the way out she saw Tina sit on his knee and jealousy flooded through her. She pretended she was going to the Ladies but hung around in the passage. The sight of them leaning over him was more than she could bear. She wanted to rush back in and yell, 'leave him. Leave him. I love him and he's mine!'

Doris was picking up the free paper from the porch where the delivery boy always chucked it. She saw Tundra's car turn into her driveway, Erica beside her. Doris was shocked, thinking of Alb's directive. She watched as Tundra took the bike out of the car, expecting Erica would wheel it round, but they both went into Number Seven.

Doris fidgeted a while, chewed the end of her apron, checked the clock, then turned down the oven where dinner was cooking, and hurried next door.

'Doris, come in.' Tundra closed the door after her.

'Well, I saw you arrive back and - '

'We're trying to locate the puncture outfit.'

'Hi, Mum. I got a flat and Mrs Tyler drove me home.' Erica was rooting in a cardboard box which Doris felt was rude of her.

'Total tip, as you see. Every time we move it's like this for weeks. Months. Years sometimes.' Tundra gave her throaty laugh, leaning against the bannister rail to light a cigarette.

'Good. Let's have a coffee.'

'I really don't think there's time - ' Doris panicked.

'Dad won't be in for another half hour. Shall I put the kettle on, Mrs Tyler?'

'Do. And call me Tundra, but only outside college, okay?'

They took their cups into the front room and Erica viewed the furnishings with a tinge of envy.

'You've got some lovely stuff.'

'Souvenirs of our travels. I always felt it helped the boys to understand other people by visiting the places they lived.' She passed them curios to handle. 'We bought those when we lived in India. That mask is Japanese. So is this fellow, a kabuki puppet. We're a magpie sort of family but I say we need beautiful objects round for inspiration.' She leaned back, blowing smoke, contemplating the sprigged wallpaper. 'I'll decorate this room as soon as poss. I expect it'll be down to Germayn and me. My other son would give a hand but he goes away a lot, touring. He periodically lives with various girlfriends then each time they break up he's back with us. He's a musician; plays saxaphone.'

She reached into a box for packets of photos. 'That's my Flex. And that's Germayn in costume. He's got a drag act in cabaret. He's doing a season at Saucy Girls here in town.'

'He must be good. I've heard it's a top venue,' said Erica. These new neighbours were an unexpected link to the world that buzzed out there, the one her father pretended didn't exist. 'Don't his legs look great in tights?'

'Men's always do,' agreed Tundra.

Doris also thought of Germayn's legs, but in connection with Alb's outburst. She gave Erica a warning look, 'we'd better go, love.'

As they came out of Number Seven the van drove up the Close. Doris gasped. To aggravate matters Alb's evening arrival ceremony had not been observed. She had unpadlocked the carport gates but they were closed. She dashed round to pull them open, lift the garage door. Alb, his engine running, watched her as she came out again and he drove in. Doris fumbled her key in the front door as Erica put her bike in the carport.

The three Wakeses went indoors. Doris scurried into the kitchen, opened the oven and looked at the, now drying, toad-in-the hole for answers. She gave a twitch as Alb followed, fists on hips. He was still in his working outfit, a sweatshirt with his employer's logo, a hammer and the name Tool Magic emblazoned on the front, the red of it amplifying his anger. Her face puckered.

'I didn't mean it to happen. You see it was, er, unavoidable. Yes. Unavoidable. I really couldn't avoid it -'

'Avoid what, Mum?' Erica came in from hanging up her coat. She saw her mother's strained attitude, the maroon temper spots on Alb's cheeks. He swung round, jabbing a finger at her.

'And you. You, what's the idea of going in there?'

'You mean next door? Well, Mrs Tyler gave me a lift

home when my bike packed up. What's wrong with that? She loaned me a puncture kit.'

'Puncture kit!' his roar rattled the grill, 'since when have we been people who borrow puncture kits? We're known for lending. That's what we do. We lend.'

'Bernardine took mine to work in her carrier. But I'll return this right now if it upsets you.' Erica shook the tin at him.

'Your mother had instructions to ignore that woman and her sons then I come home and find you both in there.'

'I-I didn't have time to tell Erica -' Doris began.

'I couldn't have complied anyway,' snapped Erica, 'Mrs Tyler happens to be a new teacher at Keggs Dell. What're you saying, Dad? I'm to ignore one of my teachers who lives next door? That won't go down well when it gets round the staff room. You're known to a lot of people.'

'Shut up. Don't dare give me lip. Useless Object.' But he was disconcerted.

'And what's the reason?' she persisted. 'What's Mrs T. supposed to have done? They only arrived yesterday and at breakfast you were all for meeting them. I think she's okay.'

Doris was trembling. Erica, although she grumbled to her mother, normally obeyed Alb's orders like the rest of them. Doris was aware of a change, a seismic shift beginning. It scared her.

'Who cares what you think. Skiving young oaf!' he bawled.

'What's wrong with them?' Erica repeated.

'I'll tell you what,' he roared, then stopped, spluttering as the humiliating scene with Tundra and Germayn came back, 'I - don't like their clothes!'

His daughter gave him an incredulous look then turned on her heel and marched upstairs.

'Come back here, you. Hey!'

The bedroom door crashed.

'You see that?' He turned to Doris, 'they're poisoning

this household already.'

She set out plates without answering. Casey popped into her head and did it for her. 'Pathetic!'

'Who, me?' asked Doris.

'No, him!'

Upstairs Erica sat on her bed, chin in hand. I knew he was mad. Doesn't like their clothes? It's as I've always thought, I've got a raving tosser for a father. Poor Mum.

Soon afterwards her elder sisters arrived home. Harriet was pondering over the remnant of gold chiffon she had in her rucksack. She planned to begin a ballgown for her best girl that evening.

Bernardine had a slightly furtive expression which nobody noticed. She slid the two bottles out of her coat pockets and took them to her tallboy. She had surprised herself by suddenly stopping as she was passing the chemist. She had gone in and bought an expensive shampoo and a conditioner. She wondered what had made her do it. Probably Erica's constant nagging. Except for Erica they all used the family sized shampoo approved on Alb's List. Her younger sister often said, 'it's all right for him. He's hardly got any hair but we need decent stuff. Specially you, Bernie, working in the open.'

As they were finishing the meal, Erica having descended in glowering silence to join them, their father announced, 'be quick and get this down then all of you into overalls.'

Erica said, 'but I can't -'

'Yes you will, lad. We're at the church hall in twenty minutes to clean and sand woodwork ready for decorating.'

When they returned much later, tired and dusty, Bernardine washed her hair as she took a shower. She shampooed it using the vat-like economy bottle bought at the supermarket. She would try the quality products another time. She would, she told herself.

CHAPTER FIVE

A thrush sang outside the window of the bathroom where Bernardine was rinsing her hair. It was half past five on an April morning two weeks later and she had finally coaxed herself to use the good shampoo and conditioner. Her movements were silent, cat-cautious, as she tried not to disturb the household. Squeezing surplus water from her head she wrapped a towel round it, tip-toed into the bedroom and slipped the incriminating bottles into a drawer. She crept downstairs with the hairdryer which she used in the scullery so no sound would reach the sleepers.

She didn't want any of them to know, couldn't stand their scrutiny. If her father found out he would sneer at her for not washing her hair in the shower, for wasting money on something of no importance. Herself. It was difficult enough to nurture the feeling she sensed growing between herself and Shaun. At least he had begun to chat when they were alone. Still no personal details had been asked or given but maybe once they were better acquainted they would get to know each other. But it would only take one of Alb's flinty remarks to demolish her hopes.

Opening the back door she took deep breaths then went into the garden. The weather had warmed it to a spring clemency and speckled it with buds. There was an energising lift of hope in her as she thought of Shaun. On impulse she pulled off her sandals and walked across the lawn, the spritzering dew brushing sparkles to her feet. She ran fingers through her damp-dry mane. Erica was right. Instead of its usual sheep's coat of a texture it had a crisp slipperiness, like the rippling surface of a leaf. As she moved it swung in an aromatic helmet round her neck.

'What d'you think you're up to, lad?' His voice scraped the quietness.

'Oh - morning, Dad.'

'Were you sleepwalking or something? It's only turned

six.' He was annoyed at being pre-empted. He was the one who always rose first in that house. 'The door was ajar. I thought we'd been burgled. And what's the idea of no shoes, you fool? If people see you they'll say you're unhinged.'

Nothing human stirred in the slumbering houses around them. The upwardly mobile couple next door, whom they rarely saw as they worked long hours all week, were obviously out of it. On the other side all Tundra's curtains were closed.

'Go and call your mother. It's time she did breakfast. And no wet footprints walked in.'

She hurried away from him. It was Saturday but they both had to go into work today. The rest of the family must also get up, of course. He had ordered them all to be at the church hall, where painting was temporarily suspended. Today was St. Chad's Spring Fair and they were helping to set up and run stalls. Afterwards they were to do home chores from a list he had made. Harriet's jobs were to clip the hedges, clean the van and everyone's shoes. Erica must accompany her mother to the supermarket, paying particular attention to choice of pickles, before doing her assignment. She no longer needed to work in Riffton library but was allowed to go to Clare's as her friend had acquired a computer. Alb readily gave permission, realising it exonerated him from any need to buy one.

Later, Erica was pleased as she and the other helpers put finishing touches to tables before the doors opened at ten. Harriet, in generous mood, had given her five pounds, a fortune in Church Fair terms. A time honoured perk of the helpers was for them to take first pick of the goods before letting loose a bargain-crazed public.

By expertly combing the clothes stalls she'd netted a haul of three decent sweaters, one only slightly wear bobbled, a cord jacket merely lacking buttons, a blouse that would go with everything. Best of all was that gem of a dress. She was lucky-dipping through sacks of donated garments when she dragged up what seemed an old, black nightie. She freed it in order to examine the clump of cardigans in which it was entangled. It looked nothing, a length of seaweed hanging from her hand. Yet something about it focused her attention. She shook it out, caught her breath when she saw who it was by.

Covering the designer label with her palm she looked round, then snatched up an unsavoury pair of vests, still sporting sepia stains under the arms. Holding the three items in a bunch she called to Mrs Copeland, who was in charge of proceedings, 'how much do I pay for these?'

Mrs Copeland, about to touch them, thought better of it, wrinkling her nose. 'Fifty pence. If you're sure you really want them?' She shot a look of distaste at the clothes, one of pity at Erica. 'No. We'll say twenty pence to you, dear.'

Once her back was turned Erica tossed the vests into the bin and put a twenty pence coin in the takings. Though it smelled of damp and stale perfume she couldn't wait to wash the dress before trying it on. Even in a creased state she saw its transforming effect on her and twirled in front of Doris.

'What d'you think, Mum?'

'Your Dad'll never allow you to put that on.' Her mother looked doubtfully at the neck revealing Erica's creamy bosom, the skirt displaying her thighs.

'He won't see me in it.'

'But when will you ever get the chance to wear it?'

'The occasion will arise. You'll see.'

The fascination people had for each other's junk at these affairs always amazed her. It wasn't only the hard up (amongst whom she counted herself), who scrabbled like hungry rats through trays of beat-up cutlery or haggled over secondhand loo seats. In the course of the morning she spotted some of the Wakes' neighbours, a couple who had a B.M.W. and a Landrover parked in their drive. There was a fierce concentration to the way they sifted through a basket of shoes, malodorous from the feet of previous owners. Catching her eye the man held up a pair of brogues in reasonable condition.

'How much to me, Erica?' He gave a disarming grin.

'All shoes are one pound fifty.'

'Discount for a friend?' (She hardly knew him).

'I can't. They're all one pound fifty.'

'But see,' said his wife, 'there's wear on one side of the soles.'

'Shall we say a quid?' the man twinkled.

'For you, one pound fifty.' Erica twinkled back at him.

They returned the shoes to the basket and walked off.

At Tool Magic Alb was fighting with a pair of taps. He stood on a step-ladder, trying to wrest them off the display stand to which they had been bolted.

'They should come out easily. Can't understand it.' He grimaced a smile at the waiting customers. They had returned a set bought last week, complaining that as soon as they'd fitted the taps and turned them on the chrome had peeled like tomato skin. The ones on display were the only set of that design in the store. Various spanners were tried unsuccessfully. The youth to whom they first applied came to Alb whose patronising, 'I'll sort this out,' was beginning to sound hollow. After twenty minutes of tugging he was forced to concede defeat.

'Excuse me a minute.' Alb, who often swore secretly to himself, went to find his boss, whom he regarded as a paranoid, jumped-up little twat, to explain the situation. The manager, annoyed at being interrupted as he was selling limed oak with brass knobs to a couple in the kitchen section, bustled over.

Enquiries as to the whereabouts of the man who had constructed the display revealed he was on holiday, his toolbox with him. In it was the only specialized wrench that could free any one of the galaxy of bathroom fittings from their peg board without breaking the expensive fixture. The manager said they could order that design of tap but it would take a week. The customers insisted they wanted it now, to put in this weekend so they could bathe. They were offered alternative designs from stock. At discount. They refused. In the end, with bad grace and muttering, they accepted a full refund.

'We can do without that,' the manager said to Alb, as though he was to blame. 'That's two customers who won't come back. Not good.'

As he walked away under a massed show of hanging lampshades, Alb threw daggers of dislike after him, wishing a shattering fall of fancy glass.

He was kept on the move all day. It was one of the busiest weekends of the year, just before Easter, the greatest festival in the D.I.Y. enthusiast's calendar. With improving daylight folk noticed the shabbiness of their decor and came for trolley loads of wallpaper and like items.

The tap incident had added vinegar to Alb's already acid temper. But there was no spleen venting permitted at work. Company policy decreed customer care a sacred priority. Every inane enquiry of, 'Where's this?', 'Where's that?', 'Do you stock dog bowls?', must be treated as if it had been made by the Queen and answered with obsequious helpfulness.

At midday there was a lull and, as he was to take a late lunch, Alb was still on duty when a call came over the intercom. Customer assistance needed at the paint mixer unit. When he got there it was deserted. Typical, they must have wandered off down another aisle. He peered round the shelf fixture.

'Here we are.' He turned to face two tall men wearing street clothes, smartish but unremarkable. Germayn, devoid of make-up, looked, if anything, more beautiful than at their first meeting. The other had a mop of well styled demi-curls, a dimple in his chin. 'Shirley bloody Temple,' flashed through Alb's mind.

'Hello, Albert. I didn't know you worked here,' said Germayn. 'Oh, I'm so glad it's you who's going to serve us.' The ghost of a snigger hung in the air but didn't materialize. 'This is my friend, Candy. She's in the same show as me.'

In trying not to snarl, Alb's face went into temporary rictus. A manicured hand was extended, forcing him to shake it.

'Pleased to meet you, Albert. Would you be a sweet boy and find me this?' Candy showed him a colour swatch taken from the rack of choices, 'that's the one we'd like, Pompidou Pearl, in vinyl silk finish.'

'Two litre size. May as well have a big one,' added Germayn. They both beamed at him, leaning flirtatiously close. He knew they were sending him up. If he could have had them in his platoon in the army for a day he'd have them sorted out. Cutting the grass with nail scissors. Cleaning the latrines with a toothbrush.

'I bet you didn't recognise me in civvies,' said Germayn. He turned to his friend. 'I'd come straight from the show, still in my gear, when I met Albert. I think he found me quite tasty.'

Alb was speechless. He snatched a two litre tin of white base from the shelf. Prized off the lid as though it was the top of Germayn's skull. He put the tin under a nozzle linked to the computer, punched in the code off the swatch and waited as the appropriate shades were squirted in.

'Ooh, that's exotic.' Candy gave an exaggerated squeal.

The back of Alb's neck prickled as they watched him put the tin inside the centrifugal mixer. As it shook and rumbled they gave delighted little groans for his benefit.

'Candy's helping me decorate my room,' Germayn volunteered. 'She has the most original notions, don't you, chuck?' He nudged his mate.

'I do.' Candy leaned an elbow on the shelf of the machine and gazed soulfully at Alb. 'I'm sensitive to the vibes around me. You must let me feng shui you some time.'

'Don't touch that thing. We're liable if the public's

harmed or get stains on themselves.' Alb pointed to a notice, then realised they'd find innuendo in what he'd said. But they didn't pick up on it as they were watching another assistant, a striking young black man, walk past. Alb took the tin out of the centrifuge and removed the lid for them to inspect the contents.

'Okay?'

'Unfortunately not.' Candy peered closely then compared it with the swatch card. 'It's the wrong one.'

Alb grabbed the card. 'It can't be.'

Germayn had a look. 'Yes, you've mixed Torque Sunset. See how much darker it is. You must've got a digit wrong in the code.'

Alb's fingers knuckled into fists. The manager would likely make him pay for his mistake. It was the fault of these two mithering him. Where, he wondered, could you get a sack of feathers? When was the last time someone got Duluxed and feathered in Manchester?

'But you know what, Cand,' Germayn looked thoughtfully at the paint, 'I like it better. Yeah, this will be more dramatic on my ceiling, extended down to the picture rail.'

'You'll still let me do the stars?'

'They'll look even better on this.' He turned back to Alb, 'I've been told you might have a ladder we can borrow. Any chance?'

'Normally I'd lend it. But it's in constant use at the church hall right now. Sorry.' He kept a whole nest of extra ladders stored in his garage roof. These two weren't coming anywhere near them.

The run-up to Easter was also frantically busy at Land o' Green as the public rediscovered its affection for gardens. There was no time during the morning for Bernardine to see Shaun as he was shuttling supplies of plants from the greenhouses to restock shelves as they emptied.

She had to do a stint on one of the shop checkouts. She found it stressful as the part-timer working the other till kept asking her the price of things at the same time that customers, a queue pressing up behind them, were asking her advice about plants they'd bought. As at Tool Magic, there was a quiet period around the lunch hour as people made for the café or the pub next door. She took a few moments to draw breath, swig a mouthful of lemonade from the can beside her. Idly she watched a car drive in to the parking strip. A woman with two young boys got out.

Bernardine tried to imagine herself wearing that suit with the short skirt. And those elegant shoes. She herself had never owned a pair with even moderately high heels. They were nice, the sort she was thinking of getting. Maybe. Well, perhaps she would. The family entered the shop and as the woman came up to her Bernardine saw she was older than herself but had a prettiness emphasized by her curtain of black hair. With an inward sigh Bernardine knew she could admire such looks but not aspire to them.

'Could you tell me where I can find Shaun Evans?' the woman asked.

Bernardine, quelling a rising unease, heard herself say, 'he's working in the greenhouses but he'll break for lunch soon.'

'Thank you. Come on, boys. We'll take a look round while we wait for Daddy.'

Bernardine went cold. More customers came to the checkout and as she worked she was aware of the little group wherever they moved, looking at things on shelves. After a while they returned to the counter and the woman paid for the novelties the boys were holding.

'Mummy, can we have one of these?' The smaller child picked up a tube of sweets from a box by the till.

'As long as you save them till after lunch.'

'I'll give some to Daddy. He likes liquorice.' They strolled out.

Her mind had gone blank. The people, the windows, the

goods around her seemed to give off an unpleasant brightness.

'I'll take over now, Bernie. You look as if you could do with something to eat.' She looked into Mr Gray's kindly face as he touched her arm, nodded, moved away. She had absolutely no appetite.

She wandered up the garden centre's private road which took in the pub before reaching the dual carriageway. As she went past she noted all the courtyard tables were occupied. It was still chilly but people sat in their coats, glad to be outdoors after the long winter. She scanned one set of customers. Walked on several paces before admitting what she'd seen, what she already knew she would see, and stopped in her tracks. The smart woman and her children were sitting there, having lunch with Shaun.

She was unable to stop herself looking back. Although she was too far away to hear their conversation their body language was unmistakable. She hadn't imagined it. They were a relaxed family group interacting together. He and the woman kept glancing up, nodding to each other as they talked.

When one of the little boys leaned against him, squeezing his arm, Shaun put it round the child, drew him close. The gesture cut through Bernardine. It was what she herself craved. The elder boy took his other arm, laughing up at him, and was also hugged. The woman said something, passed Shaun a tissue with which he wiped the child's nose. Then he got up and went into the pub, to pay the bill, Bernardine presumed.

When he came out she had concealed herself behind a spreading forsythia, coming mockingly into bloom. She peered obsessively through the blossoms as the pair of them walked to the car, holding the children's hands. He settled them in the back seat, leaned in to kiss them. Every action moved him further and further from her, tearing off part of her in the process.

The woman got into the driver's seat and brushed her

hair back. She looked up and he bent his head towards her. Bernardine knew he would kiss her too. She shut her eyes tightly, compressed her mouth to keep in the scream.

She trudged round the tree plantation, trying to dull the pain. What a fool she'd been, she berated herself. It was her own fault for being stupid, imagining things that were never there. She'd misread his friendly manner for interest in her. He'd never said he wasn't married and she'd never asked. They hadn't discussed their home life, their backgrounds. When they were together she blocked out thoughts of her family. With Shaun she felt she was becoming another person. But all those things said at home must be right after all. The Bernardine who lived in Turvey Close was the real one, the unattractive one. The one she didn't like. The one Shaun didn't love.

She somehow crawled through the rest of the day, operating on automatic, outwardly normal. When she got back to Number Nine she went to her room, closing the door against the others. Harriet, when she came to bed, knew better than to speak to her sister. All night Bernardine lay sleepless, listening to a fierce wind that had got up unexpectedly, scouring the gardens of tender plants, ripping at the burgeoning trees.

On Sunday afternoon she was working in the garden when Alb joined her. His presence was an irritation.

'Bernard, look,' he accused, pointing to an acer which was her present to him on his last birthday. 'It was in bud but now see the leaves. They've shrivelled at the edges. Well? What is it?'

'I'm not sure.' She couldn't concentrate on the plant for the misery dragging her insides.

'Huh! The so-called educated member of this family's not sure. Three years of sacrifice I made to send you to the Rural Studies Centre. What was all that about?'

Dully she bent nearer. 'It can't be leaf curl, that takes

longer to develop and it was fine yesterday. When I go into work I'll ask their advice. Mr Gray is bound to know. Or - or Shaun.'

She couldn't help his name slipping out but speaking it in her father's presence caused a spasm of guilt. Shaun seemed to have stepped out of her mind to stand beside them on the lawn.

'You'd better. If it can't be cured get me another. The same colour, mind.'

She wondered if he had any idea what the little Japanese shrub had cost, even with staff discount.

'Okay, Dad.'

'Give me a hand with the seedlings.' He opened the greenhouse and she followed him into the humid space. He passed her a stack of small clay pots. 'There's time to repot all of these before we set off for your Grandma's.'

'Grandma's? What for?'

'Dimmer than usual today, aren't you, lad.' He thrust a bony wrist under her nose, tapped his watch dial. 'The date; see the date? Does the date mean anything to you? It's the anniversary of the Fall. When my Father, your Grandfather, God-rest-him, passed on. A fat lot you care if you've forgotten.'

'It's not that. Mum did mention, I...I' But she had forgotten. What went on lately at Number Nine happened in a haze of voices, footsteps, misty faces. The only image clearly in focus was of Shaun and the black haired woman, leaning towards each other. She couldn't prevent herself playing it over and over, each time giving another twist to an inward knot of pain.

'And tidy yourself up before we go. Try and look respectable instead of a scarecrow. Your head's a bird's nest. I keep telling you, get a haircut, man.'

Accustomed not to react, show emotion, she concentrated on the task in hand as he continued to criticize. Without warning something boiled up and the lid kept on her feelings blew off. She bent in two, shaken with

85

harsh sobs, saltwater rushing and dripping from her into the pot she held. It fell to the floor, smashed, scattering soil over the scrubbed boards.

'What've you done?' he shouted. This was never Bernard.

She rushed away from him into the house. He followed, gaping in consternation. 'Bernard, where d'you think you're going?'

'To take Miss Spencer's dog for a walk,' she choked. She ran out of the front door, slamming it. Alb came out after her and stood watching as she marched, tight-shouldered, down the Close towards the elderly neighbour who lived on the main road.

'Be back at half past five,' he called, with a semblance of good humour, mindful of surrounding windows.

CHAPTER SIX

At half past six, when Bernardine still hadn't returned he was furious. 'This is flagrant disrespect. What do I say to Mother? She'll think Bernard doesn't want to visit her on such an important occasion.'

Dead right, thought Erica. Just like the rest of us. Aloud she suggested, 'Dad, we can say Bernardine's had to work today, that someone from the nursery's off ill?'

He rounded on her. 'Lie to your Grandmother? Oh, that's nice. Seventeen years in a decent home, water off a duck's back to you.' He turned to Doris, 'I was under the impression you'd raised Christians.' He spoke as though she'd planted carrots and sprouts had come up. 'This lot have had it too soft. Cushy. My Mother had a cure for lying. She'd wash out our mouths with carbolic.'

As he spoke an involuntary shudder went up his back. He tasted again the burning chemical sensation on his tongue. Tears and mucus running painfully back up his nose, into his mouth as his face was pressed into the bucket of soapy water she'd just used to swill the floor. His gurgling screams protested that it wasn't him. It wasn't him. He didn't take the biscuits. He didn't. But she had punched him hard in the chest where the crumbs on his shirt betrayed him. As she finished scouring his mouth with the nailbrush and dragged him up for air he caught sight of his brother, calmly watching his humiliation, as usual.

'He took them. He ate them too.' Alb had blubbered, 'I got them off him.'

'Don't try putting the blame on George. He doesn't steal. He's a good boy.' The blow this time was between his shoulders. It made him see stars.

Taking the belt she kept hanging on a hook for the purpose, she beat him round the kitchen then threw him into the cupboard under the stairs where his crying was too muffled to disturb them.

Now Alb paced up and down the living room. Warily silent, the three women watched him. Everyone was dressed somberly, he in dark suit and tie, Doris in a grey dress, the girls in their churchwear. This ritual of Grandfather's anniversary stretched back as far as Erica could remember. A kind of weird birthday that wasn't, for someone they had never met who held a mythical status in the family. As they waited for her father to simmer down she held a box wrapped in fancy paper. Grandma's annual tribute.

'We can still go, Dad,' murmured Harriet. 'I mean, Grandma will be even more annoyed if none of us turns up.'

'No choice, is there?' He jangled the van keys. 'There's never been less than the five of us. Even that year your mother had 'flu and I had to make her sit in the next room so Mother wouldn't get infected, I made sure we all turned up. I'll have something to say to that party later when he comes in.'

Doris got into the passenger seat while Harriet and Erica folded themselves in the back of the van as best they could. There was a bit of carpet on the floor but the sides pressed hard against them as they went round corners and over every spine jarring bump in the road. When they were being used as labourers on a project the van was always full of tools so they followed on bikes, which was far more comfortable.

The van had been bought in preference to a car not only because it was cheaper but it enabled Alb to gain virtue points by obliging the vicar or neighbours in transporting items here and there, picking up logs, taking their old mattresses to the tip. As he drove he usually played country and western tapes but now he held a stony silence. For the three mile journey nobody spoke.

His mother, Lily, had grown up in the Ladybarn area, not far from the city centre. Of her six brothers and sisters she was the only survivor, tuberculosis having claimed the rest. It was feared she herself would go the same route so she became the centre of attention to anxious parents. They drove themselves to give her as much as they could afford. Often what they couldn't. First choice of whatever clothes, sweets, fruit in season, always went to their cherished daughter. When she was grown, a local painter and decorator, Len Wakes, who succumbed to her charms, was made to understand, both by Lily and her parents, what a prize he'd secured. He thought himself privileged and continued the tradition.

They rented a small house near her parents, whose death a few years later knocked the pedestal from under her. With three children to raise on Len's limited income Lily was dismayed to find her indulgences severely curtailed. It was a home where there was never enough of anything, especially food. Where toilet paper was torn up squares of the *Daily Mirror* threaded on string, and gaps in the soles of shoes were often lined with cardboard.

Being hard up was the normal condition of eveyone else they knew. Yet Lily had a way of conveying to her family that she was a cut above the sordid struggle, deserved something finer and they were to blame for her not getting it. Alb remembered his father as a worried looking man, always doing improvements round the house, or bringing home small luxuries to try to please his mother, and failing to do so. Nothing ever quite satisfied her.

The big change came when Alb was fourteen. His father, painting the frame of a skylight in the roof of Porton's Bakeries Ltd, leaned on a rotten timber which gave way. Plummeting to the floor, forty feet below, he hit a steel-topped table on the way, his blood mingling with the flour, his skull as smashed as the Cornish pasties onto which he crashed.

During the next three years Lily and her children descended to a grimmer poverty. Often meals were skipped entirely or replaced with cups of Oxo to deceive their stomachs. Fortunately the children were kept going on one free school lunch a day during term.

As the eldest, Alb was already doing a paper round but now took on all sorts of extra jobs. The minute he turned sixteen Lily took him out of school and sent him to work in a wood merchant's. Evenings he served in a chip shop. Although his brother was only two years younger it appeared George could not be spared to go out to work. George was clever at school so his studies took priority. Alb was permanently tired and when he did lie down was too exhausted to sleep properly.

Then, when it seemed things could get no worse, the union lawyers working on her case won Lily an out of court settlement. In her terms it was a sum to rival a football pools win. Friends urged a move to a country cottage. Somewhere in Cheshire, maybe Cheadle Hulme or Altrincham? No, too posh with all those trees and black and white beams. Derbyshire then? But Lily knew better, opting to stay a short bus ride from the old district. It meant she could go to the same shops, church and bingo club she knew. More importantly, she could swank to the same neighbours, let them witness her move to her rightful position, in a road where all the houses were individually designed.

The van drew up outside Flower Baskets, a hacienda style bungalow. The said baskets hung along the stucco though it was too early in the year for anything but ivy to fill them. Alb's rap on a brass pixie was answered by his brother, looking solemn.

'Hello, George.' Alb assumed an identical demeanour.

'Come in, Albert. Come in, dears,' he beckoned the women. Then, as they followed his waddling figure down the hall, he lowered his voice, 'she's in the lounge. Quite upset, you know. Been talking about the past.'

Here we go again, thought Erica as they entered the chandeliered room and filed across a desert of fitted carpet.

Next to the fire Lily sat in a high armchair wearing an aspect of melancholy and clutching a glass of gin. She wore an expensive black suit, antique jet earrings; shoes, stockings, even her watch strap was black. Above the fireplace in a black frame hung a portrait of Len Wakes, badly executed in oils by a local art student commissioned to copy it from a photo. More of these were dotted over the walls. Also in the room sat three of Lily's old neighbours who had been around when the original event occurred and came for the yearly replay.

'Mother, how are you?' Alb stepped up to peck her cheek and the rest of his family, following the set form, did likewise.

'Thinking of the Fall, Albert. As always, I had the vicar do the prayers for his anniversary in church this morning. Ooh, it all comes back on this day.'

Because you make sure of that. Erica suppressed a shudder as she kissed her grandmother's face that put her in mind of imitation leather worn thin. She could visualize the wrinkles splitting open any minute to reveal a woven backing material. Grey eyeshadow gave Lily's cadaverous face a sinister look. Her stare was a pair of bluebottles darting over them. For a moment she and Erica eyeballed each other in mutual dislike before Harriet replaced her sister in the homage queue.

Lily suddenly asked, 'where's the other one got to?'

'Ah,' Alb was apologetic, 'I'm sorry, Mother. Taken ill, I'm afraid. Probably ate something that didn't agree.' That, he excused himself, could account for Bernard's crazy behaviour. Lily's mouth pleated and straightened as she gave him a scowl. He fidgeted, embarrassed. He went on, 'gastric problem. Wouldn't want to mess up the Anniversary with someone throwing up in your nice house.'

'I'll believe you where thousands wouldn't.' She used the sarcastic phrase remembered from his childhood. She turned to the other old women who looked down their noses at him and nodded knowingly. He flushed, then, taking the box from Erica, passed it to his mother with a flourish.

'A gift to cheer you up, Mother. I hope you'll like it.'

Exactly the same words every year. The ritual. Erica ground her teeth.

'Thank you, Albert. But nothing can take the sorrow away. It's always there.' With sad efficiency Lily ripped off the wrapping, pulled at the lid, and, when it stuck, clawed the box open. She lifted out a china lady whose crinoline and ringlets were frozen in mid-swirl.

'I know you don't have that one because it's an exclusive design released on the market this year.' Intently, hungrily, he was watching her. 'It's bigger than the ones I've given you before but, well, you deserve it.'

The amount spent on that thing could've gone towards a lap-top or a secondhand PC Erica frowned to herself. Some hope. Alb had seen the ornament advertised on the back page of a magazine. A full colour photograph of 'Delphiana' had insets showing details of the modelling of the hands and parasol, the real crystal on each shoe. It could be bought for thirty pounds down with further installments for the same amount paid over the next ten months.

'She's one of a limited edition of only two thousand by an award-winning artist. They break the mould, you know. The edging on her clothes is hand painted twenty two carat gold.' He reached for it, 'shall I put her with the others?' On the far wall was a display cabinet crammed with posturing ceramic women.

'Sit down, Albert. All of you.' With an unintentional curtsey they sank on to the velvet suite. Lily put on her glasses, held the figurine, turning it this way and that, examining it closely. She remembered to sop her eyes with a lace hankie every few seconds, sighing deeply as Erica watched the performance with disgusted fascination.

'See, George?' Lily turned to her other son.

'Really, really lovely, Mother,' he agreed in his creaking

treble. 'That's a very nice item you've brought, Albert.'

The thin curve of Alb's smile appeared as George handled the figurine, his beady gaze admiring.

'Thank you very much, Albert. Put it in the cabinet,' ordered Lily. 'There's space on the bottom shelf, although I've had to move some of my ladies to make room for what George gave me.'

Halfway across the vista of carpet Alb stopped in mid stride, staring at a large china group that now held pride of place. It was the Queen, sitting side-saddle on a horse, every detail intricately defined, down to the buckles on the harness.

'It's Her Majesty Trooping The Colour.' Lily's mouth chumbled as though it savoured the taste of banknotes. 'Those first came out in the Fifties, soon after the Coronation. I was dying to have one. I was in tears because I wanted it so much. That upset your father but of course it was beyond his means, although he tried, God-rest-him. Afterwards people wouldn't sell. Everyone realised they'd be antiques of the future. Now they're collectors' pieces. Real collectors' pieces.'

Alb cleared his throat several times, cocking his head to look at the Queen. His complexion had taken on the mottling of a slice of Spam, an ominous sign recognised by Doris and the girls.

'Very handsome,' his voice was a croak. 'Yes. Very well made. Good.'

He opened the cabinet, placed the crinoline woman inside then quickly withdrew his hand as if it had been burnt. George came to stand beside him, viewing the exhibits with his yellowed smile.

'I'd had a sizeable bonus and, as you say, Mother deserves the best. A friend in the antiques trade put me in touch with a specialist dealer.'

Erica made a swift change of subject, 'have you heard from Aunt Sylvia lately, Grandma?'

'She sent those, Interflora.' Lily indicated a bunch of

roses amounting to a bush. 'She's doing very well working in what they call real estate over there. Todd's taken her and the boys to their beach house at the minute. Bring me the photos, George.'

'Why don't we look at them after supper, dear, after we've drunk Dad's Toast? Shall we all go through?'

Lily set down her glass and, with a low, despairing moan, gripped the arms of the chair, struggling to rise to her feet. Her two sons plunged forward simultaneously, seized an elbow each, levered her upright. They walked her tenderly to the dining room followed by the attendant neighbours, Doris and the girls. Harriet suppressed a grin as Erica made faces at their grandmother's scrawny back. Lily famously bus-tripped off to York or Blackpool for the day every month. She went on regular five hour shopping sprees into town or the Trafford Centre, went sequence dancing at a pensioners' club on Monday nights. But now she was putting her all into the annual performance of stricken widowhood. She was guaranteed the spotlight before an audience blackmailed to attend. And there was something for her to genuinely celebrate. In his life Len never fulfilled her expectations, but by dying gave her all she wanted. She threw out one or two dodders and an inspired quiver before they sat her at the table.

Erica gazed on it with horrified admiration. She'd surpassed herself this year. All the crockery was black, arranged round a black vase of florist's funeral lilies against which leaned another photo of Grandad, this time in a silver frame embossed with mourning angels. It was flanked by black candles in ebony-effect holders. His wartime service medals were set out on a small sable cushion. There was even a set of modern cutlery with black handles. Erica wondered if somewhere in the city there was an undertakers' cash-and-carry mart that her grandmother frequented.

George filled the glasses which they then raised, 'To Len', 'To Dad', 'To Grandad.' Over the spread of dainties there was a prolonged retrospective discussion of the times of Lily and Len. Then Lily's glance raked the other Wakes females.

'This makes the few years I've got left more pleasant, having family visit me. Even if it takes a sad occasion to prompt them.'

'Er, Alb and the girls have been terribly busy for weeks, Mother,' Doris explained, 'doing work for the church.'

'Yes. Remember I told you, Mother, we had a new vicar taking over? Mr Coulson, an excellent man. First rate. He says, well -' Alb looked down modestly, 'he says I've been wonderful helping him settle into the parish.'

Lily didn't respond but looked Harriet up and down. 'You don't put any more meat on your bones do you, lass?' She turned to the crones, 'I'm convinced she'll stay an Olive Oyl the rest of her life, meself. She takes after Albert.' She assessed Erica, 'whereas you're the opposite, chuck. Used to be a little elf when you were younger. Getting a bit on the porkish side now though.' She clicked her tongue, 'you should watch it. You youngsters go stuffing yourselves with chips and before you know it you're sixteen stone.'

'Big thighs,' nodded one of her friends. 'That's where it settles.'

'She'll end up having her stomach stapled when she's older, if she's not careful,' agreed another.

'Erica's not overweight. They're both in proportion.' Doris was goaded into saying.

'Now don't take offence, chuck. I didn't mean anything. I'm just taking an interest in my grandchildren.' Lily's patting hand snaked across her sleeve. 'You shouldn't upset yourself, not with twitchy nerves like yours. What is it you take for them now?'

'She doesn't, Mother,' answered Alb. 'We cured her of all that nervous business a while back. Don't you recall, I told you we'd got her right with the power of prayer? The receptionists at our local surgery are in St. Chad's prayer group. They kept a kindly eye on her, prevented her asking the doctor for more pills. She's right as rain now.'

Doris had the conviction that she was becoming transparent. She was fading into her chair, disappearing into the background and soon wouldn't be here any more. She tried to call up Casey but there was no response. Then Erica squeezed her arm.

'More tea, Mum?'

'It's bad manners to offer people things when you aren't the hostess,' snapped Lily.

'And as Uncle George is pouring it'd be daft not to let him know, wouldn't it?' Erica retorted. 'I'll have another while you're at it, please, Uncle.'

She clattered the cups over to George and for several seconds an equilateral triangle of glaring formed between Erica and her father and grandmother. Lily looked as if she'd like to hit her with the black-glazed teapot.

Bernardine had walked for miles, talking to the dog about life's injustice. She did a round trip through the top of the country park that stretched to the environs of the city, arriving back at the gates in Riffton as dusk fell. It wasn't wise to be among the trees at the hour when other dogwalkers had gone and muggers emerged with the owls and foxes. She delivered the dog back to his owner, then continued tramping the streets, loath to return to Turvey Close, desperate for relief from the strangulating ache in her.

She went in the opposite direction to the estate, struck out along the streets of tall older houses. It was impossible to resist glancing in lit windows, snatching kaleidescopic slivers of other lives. The corner of a kitchen cabinet with pans on it in an attic bedsit, a row of books on a sill, a child flying paper arrows to his sister, people in conversation on a couch. At an open door a woman brushing a step looked up as she went past. Inside someone called and there was an answering laugh.

She was aware of something organic, unstoppable, happening all around. That force she saw in her plants. She yearned to be absorbed by it, felt herself surrounded but excluded by it. Just by being himself Shaun was part of this, but she wasn't. She felt an ugly mesh of unworthiness covering her whole person. She was a grotesque female who had no right to love anyone.

She told herself she wouldn't even imagine herself competing with other women, not Sue and Tina, certainly not the likes of Shaun's wife. She wouldn't be a fool any more. She'd concentrate on work. On what she knew, what got results. She stopped and pressed knuckles to her midriff, taking deep, searing breaths. But he'd changed all that, hadn't he? It wasn't possible to lose herself amongst the plants any more. Everything she did, everywhere she moved, his face was before her.

She wandered foggily past the library, the health centre. She hardly registered an hysterical wail of sirens on the nearby main road. Leaning against the wall of a building she recognised the funeral parlour. She trudged round to the front and looked at it, just recognisable as the cinema it had been. It was where a famous pop group of singing brothers, who lived close by as youngsters, played their first gig. From a place of fun and song to death's resting house. Yes, she agreed with herself, it fitted her mood perfectly. She window-shopped the tombstones displayed. What would be written on hers? Nothing. They wouldn't think she was worth forking out cash for. She worked with earth and would end up as a heap of it.

Looking up she noticed a disturbance a block further on. Where the two main roads through Riffton crossed, a small crowd had gathered as motor cycle police cordonned off the road outside the building society, unusually ablaze with lights on a Sunday. There were police cars flashing, an ambulance into which two figures were being stretchered. A security vehicle was slewed across the pavement at an angle. Bernardine gulped. Probably another raid. Life was so horrible. For some people only destruction and pointless misery waited.

It started to drizzle and she hastened away from the scene, back towards Turvey Close. The rain got heavier and became a penetrating deluge battering at her. She started to run, was soaked within minutes. Earlier she'd dashed out coatless, wearing a canvas gilet she used for gardening because of its many pockets. Now it became a sponge that held water onto her skin.

She ran faster, trying to ward off the cold, seized with the thought of getting home, into dry things before the family returned. Coin-sized raindrops bounced off the drive as she sprinted up it, reached the porch. Then realised she had no key. The porch was locked, of course, as were the iron gates to the carport. She pressed herself against them, seeing into the protected space she couldn't reach, feeling utterly defeated. A wave of grief overwhelmed her.

Tundra, putting out milk bottles, heard weeping from the other side of the hedge, grabbed an umbrella and went to investigate.

'What's the matter, love?'

Bernardine felt a hand on her shoulder. Through tear bloated eyes she saw her towering neighbour holding a golf umbrella over her.

'Compost,' sobbed Bernardine, 'it's all I'm fit for. Compost.'

'Not for a while yet. Forgotten your key, have you? Come along.'

Spent with emotion, Bernardine, sagging at the knees, trying to explain, was propelled down the path and into next door.

'Off with the boots and clothes. They're saturated.'

'But I couldn't, Mrs Tyler -'

'Hold still while I undo this for you.'

She was too weak to protest as Tundra peeled the wet things from her. Bernardine's teeth were chattering so much she didn't have time to be embarrassed as she was whizzed, naked, up the stairs, enveloped in a large dressing gown. Tundra went into the bathroom, turned taps on.

'There are the towels. While you take a hot soak I'll tumble dry your stuff.'

Bernardine obeyed. Bemused, she climbed into the bath, lay in the soothing warmth with a sense of unreality. Everything had happened so quickly. It was bizarre to have this neighbour she hardly knew take charge of her. And the older woman's great size increased her own illusion of being a child again.

When she came downstairs in the dressing gown Tundra sat her beside a crackling fire with a mug of chocolate. Lighting a cigarette she lowered herself onto the chair opposite, regarding her visitor.

'Feeling better, I see. You're the eldest, Bernardette?'

'Bernardine. Oh, Mrs Tyler, you've been so kind. I'm sorry to be a nuisance.'

'You've given an unexpected frisson to a quiet evening, love. I was only setting a project for my class. Now, d'you want to say what's upset you?'

'It was getting caught in the wet, being locked out. I'm such an idiot.'

'Okay, if you don't want to discuss it. Your clothes should be dry now.' She fetched them from the kitchen. 'Put them on here. Everyone's out but me.'

Bernardine felt it would be rude to refuse but her habitual shyness rose to the surface, making her flush. As she struggled into her things before this stranger, trying not to expose her hateful body, Tundra didn't avert her gaze but watched quite openly. She said, 'you'll need to stay here until your family gets back so I may as well sketch you. If you don't object?'

'Er, no.' She shook her head, taken aback. For the first time she noticed the canvasses stacked in corners, paintings on the walls and propped against them.

Tundra sat with a sketchblock on the plateau of her knee, working in pencil. She moved swiftly, peeling off each sheet as it was finished, putting it aside. She moved her reluctant model to different positions, standing her up at one point. Then she changed to drawing with charcoal on paper pinned to a board.

'All right? Not getting stiff?'

'I'm fine, thanks, Mrs Tyler.' It was true. There was something calming about this big woman in her comfortable room. At last Tundra was finished.

'Could I - see them?'

She stared at the drawings. She always shied away from thinking about how she looked. The truth was she didn't really know. It was impossible to judge without input other than her father's barbs, her mother's pale reassurance, Harriet's crazy suggestions. How could she be this woman dominating the page with her sinuous body, her mass of hair? Did she look out at the world this way, from this unimagined face?

'One of my ex-husbands was partial to your type. He'd have termed you a fine figure of a woman. Keep that if you like.'

'Thank you. Thank you. I wish I could draw.' She looked up at Tundra whose green eyes held shrewdness, friendliness. Found herself saying, 'it was something in work that shook me.'

'A row or a bloke?'

'A bloke,' she hesitated, 'Shaun.'

And in the tranquil parlour, aglow with ethnic wall hangings, cushions, and plants, Bernardine was able, for the first time in her life, to tell another person how she really felt.

Later, when the rain had stopped, they heard the van. Bernardine used a bin sack to protect her from the wet hedge as she squeezed through to the back of Number Nine. She hung about outside the window and when Doris came to close the curtains, signalled to her. Her mother put a finger to her lips, pointing upwards. Alb had gone to the bathroom. Doris opened the back door and gave her daughter a questioning look. Bernardine shook her head and shot upstairs. She made it into her room as she heard the lavatory flush.

As he and Doris got ready for bed Alb was still fuming. He had banged on the door shouting, 'Bernard. Get out here. I want a word with you.' But, to his disbelief, she ignored him. Harriet opened the door to convey the unlikely message that her sister was asleep. He couldn't bring himself to enter the room. Behind Harriet he was confronted by the wall covered with row upon row of those rampant icons of femininity. The tiny, smiling faces and pert busts of the massed teendolls were pointed at him with a sneer. He seethed with murderous things he would say at breakfast.

Doris felt anger pulsating from him as they lay in bed. He ranted at her in the dark about how that lad's behaviour had spoiled the evening for everyone. Doris knew what had really done it was the Queen Trooping The Colour. Then he went quiet and she felt a familiar apprehension. The bony piston of his arm came over her. It was as she had feared. She took a surreptitious swipe of Vaseline from the jar she kept ready on the bedside table.

'Right then, Dor,' his voice was warmer. But brisk, as if they were about to share a task. He slid his pyjama trousers off, dropped them on the floor, neatly raised her nightdress in folds, like a window blind.

Doris realised the term 'screwing' was an impolite description vulgar people used for the sexual act. However, it seemed so apt in describing Alb's attentions to herself. Before he had bought a rechargeable power tool he'd used a manual ratchet screwdriver for D.I.Y. jobs. As he put on his condom under the duvet she sensed his concentration, as when changing the bit, placing it carefully. And he performed the activity itself with the same series of rhythmic thrusts she had so often witnessed as he drove a screw into a rawplug to hang a wall fitment.

She always found it scarey once he got a momentum going. He gripped her tightly, as if she were about to escape. She hung on to him, with an irrational conviction his brain or bottom could burst if he got too overwrought. She regarded these bouts as a kind of fit Alb was seized by from time to time, which it was her duty to get him through. He seemed to go temporarily off his head and accompanied the D.I.Y. gestures with a continual grunt of, 'numf, numf, numf.' Getting faster he then ended on the note, 'numfnumfnumf-ah-ah-ahrgh!' After a short respite of breathing himself back to normal he turned over and went to sleep.

As always Doris lay awake, staring into the dark. She was filled with an odd, weepy achiness she couldn't define. As though there was something she should have had which never arrived.

CHAPTER SEVEN

Next morning it was raining, the grey of the day corresponding to the atmosphere round the table. Alb gnashed out a grace then, as everyone ate their toast, launched into a tirade against Bernardine. She didn't answer but continued spreading marmalade as though he were a voice on the radio.

'- and my Mother, your poor Grandmother, was devastated. Devastated. How could you snub a frail old lady whose only interest in life is her family? Do you want to kill her?'

'D'you want them scrambled or boiled?' Doris whispered to Erica.

'To let her down on such a day. You have no feelings.'

'Boiled, please.'

'Fried for me.' Harriet chipped in.

'Eggs!' He turned his attention to them, 'your Grandma struggled to give us eggs, but we could only have dripping for breakfast. And glad of it. I hardly recognised an egg till I was twelve. Anyone who owned a hen was somebody then.' He turned back to Bernardine, 'your conscience should be pricking for running out on us, you heartless oaf.'

'Ham and sweetcorn all right, Alb?' Doris was making sandwiches for their lunchpacks as she watched the eggs cook.

'And sliced onion on it. How many times must I tell you?'

'Cheese and tomato, please, Mum,' said Bernardine.

'Oh. Oh. Got a tongue when you want something. You owe me an apology, lad.'

'Sorry!' She flung the word like a wet dishcloth in his face. He glowered. There was something different about her. Usually when he scolded she hunched her shoulders, dropped her gaze. Now she merely looked sullen.

'Can you put in a Kit-Kat, Mum?' asked Erica. Alb gave his bitter laugh.

'Kit-Kat! I was lucky if I saw one at Christmas.'

And got a carrot in the toe of a sock, lard to rub on our boils for a treat, Erica silently added.

They were interrupted by the clack of the letterbox. Doris fetched the mail and handed him a sheaf of bills which set him off again.

'More demands for money. It costs a fortune to keep this roof over you lot. I slog my guts out, and for what?'

As they were leaving everyone pecked Doris on the cheek but only Erica noticed her mother's face had a sickly pallor.

'Mum, are you okay? She enclosed Doris in a crackle of waterproof sleeves, 'you look ill.'

'What do you know? Of course she's all right, aren't you, Dor? Now get going or you'll be late for college.'

'I'm fine, Erica love. Bye.'

It was only after they'd gone that Doris stood alone in the kitchen pressing a fist to her mouth. Horrified.

By the time Harriet reached the warehouse where she worked the weather had brightened. Wheeling her bike through a side door she parked it with others in a passage, took off her wet cagoule and picked her way past stacked bales and boxes into the public area. A fresh delivery was being unpacked and, catching a shimmer of silver, she hurried to help.

'Nice, eh?' Her boss had unrolled several metres of the material and draped it over a display rack. 'It's insulation stuff left over from that posh hotel they've built by the canal.'

'You could do all sorts with it,' Harriet fingered the gritty yet supple texture. 'Angel wings. An underwater scene.'

He nodded, 'or a science fiction thing. Take over, will you, Harriet.'

She enjoyed working at Spraffy's, which was officially a City Play Resource Facility For Youth, a registered charity with both voluntary and paid workers, such as herself. The aim was to provide resource materials cheaply to aid child development. An Aladdin's cave of toys, games, craft items at discounted rates, it also carried massive amounts of scrap material donated by businesses in the city, ends of rolls, surplus stock, stickyback plastic, card tubes.

Spraffy's also did a swap and exchange system with similar Scrapstores round the country so, among other things, there was a constant flow of exciting and beautiful cloth going in and out, delectable offcuts to be gleaned. It was a situation ideal for an employee with several hundred teendolls to dress.

'Harriet.' She turned, recognising the youth worker whom she had helped to costume an amateur production of *West Side Story.* 'I popped in to give you a couple of comps for the opening night. You should come and see the results of your work on stage.'

'Thanks, Sarah. I'd love to. I'll do my best to be there.' Harriet looked longingly at the tickets in her hand. Customers often gave her complimentaries but she was rarely able to use them. Her father always found a reason why she couldn't go.

Although the small staff were expected to pitch in on any job Harriet's sewing skills meant most of her time was spent in the costume department. Along with the likes of bouncy castles and unicycles, Spraffy's hired out costumes for events and promotions, and were often asked to make them for plays. It was what she liked best, interacting with the teachers and youth leaders who asked her advice, but the drama groups were her favourites. Occasionally, professional actors came in and, as she pinned and tacked, she listened to snippets of theatrical gossip, wishing she could belong to that world.

As none of her colleagues were over-keen on sewing Harriet had taken over Costumes as her domain; improving herself, developing her own ideas, getting pattern books through the library. And, of course, there was the pleasure of first testing her designs in miniature on her girls at home.

At lunchtime Ann came in from the nearby office where she worked. As usual, they shared sandwiches in the staff room and Harriet showed her the tickets.

'You may as well have them, see if you can find someone to take.' Of course Ann would be free to see the show.

'I'll not go without you. Let's think if we can work it.' Familiar with Alb's vindictiveness she pondered on how they could petition him.

'We're painting the inside of the church hall now. I know he'll use it as an excuse to say I can't be spared.'

'Tell you what,' Ann suggested, 'I'll get my dad to ring him. Yours listens to him.'

'It's worth a try,' Harriet was doubtful. 'Let's go see what's new.'

Together they inspected the stock. Ann pounced on tubes of tiny beads. 'Perfect for Guinevere's bodice.'

Harriet nodded. Ann's collection of teendolls, though not so large as her own, was slightly grander as she could always afford new ones, plus their accessories. However, like herself, Ann also spent hours making outfits for them and was currently robing a group of Action men and Barbies as characters from Camelot.

Originally it was Ann who told Harriet a job was going at Spraffy's. Alb opposed her application because she was already an assistant in a dry cleaners. But two things conspired to change his mind. First, Ann's father praised the establishment as an asset to the community, something Alb smugly identified with. Then another worker from the dry cleaners appeared in the local paper. He had been arrested for indecent exposure in a Post Office where, after sticking stamps to his anatomy, he shouted to the clerk, 'look, missis - how's that for First Class?'

'Anyway, Dor,' Alb said later, in Harriet's hearing, 'this job'll suit our Harry, I suppose. Sounds like it doesn't need anyone too bright.'

The women combed the shelves for treasure. Rooting through a box Harriet lifted a roll of material, 'wow, look at this.' She unwound it, arranging it jokily round her friend. 'I must have it.'

'It's wild. But isn't that fuchsia pink too harsh for the girls? What could you use it for?'

Harriet wasn't sure. At home she had drawers full of such remnants, sequins, feather boas. This glamorous piece of fabric must join them. Their day of usefulness would come. She didn't know how or why but felt it in her bones.

Doris hugged the tray of plants to her and glanced at her watch. There was time before Alb appeared. Oh, why had Tundra been late back from college this evening? She had just seen her neighbour arrive home and she needed to go to her. She must. She scurried up the path of Number Seven but Germayn answered her knock.

'Hello. Is Tundra around?'

'Mumzo's in the loo but come in and wait if you like.'

'No,' Doris was ready to weep, 'I only thought she might like some primroses for the stone planter.'

'That's ever so kind. Thanks.' He took them from her, saw her agitation. 'Doris, are you okay? Is something up?'

'I'm fine, thanks.'

'You don't look it. Do step in.' He opened the door wider.

'I can't. I -' She wanted to blurt it out to this concerned looking young man. 'I must go. I've something cooking.'

Despairingly she returned to her house.

At dinner Alb said to Harriet, 'Councillor Jones rang me today. To ask if you'd care for a lift to some show with Ann.' She tried not to look hopeful. 'I had to say no. I explained you're needed on Church business this Thursday.'

'But it's only one evening, Dad. I promise I'll make it up.' A token try.

'No. It's bad enough now with Rick skiving off twice a week to his mate's.'

'Erica goes there for college work,' Doris murmured. 'Making use of Clare's computer saves her waiting for time

107

on the library ones, Alb. You've told her practice is important.'

'And it's important for me not to offend good customers when they invite me to their shows.' Harriet spoke with a flash of annoyance.

'Be quiet,' shouted Alb. 'You're not leaving it all to me and Bernard to do. The matter's closed.'

Bernardine ignored them all. She stared at her plate then got up and went to her room.

'What's up with that fool?' He frowned after her.

'Bernardine's, er, never been keen on shepherd's pie.' Doris tried to speak soothingly but her own mind was in turmoil. She wished Erica was here. Her youngest daughter was always the most supportive of any of them, but dare she be told the secret? She might let it slip to her father the next time they rowed.

'Dor, didn't you hear me? I said you can give me another helping.'

'Sorry, Alb.' Trying to keep a steady hand she did as he asked. God, she thought fearfully, what will happen? He'll go raving mad when he finds out what I've done.

In reality Erica hadn't done much computing on the evenings she'd escaped to Clare's. It was true that Clare's father, a man besotted with technology, had bought himself a state-of-the-art Macintosh and passed his discarded model to his daughter, who lived in hope that he would do the same with his car.

At the time that the Wakeses were finishing off shepherd's pie the two girls were in Clare's bedroom, encasing their busts in papier mache. It was part of Tundra's art project and, though Erica wasn't on her course she felt justified in joining in as she was being used as one of the models and found it more entertaining anyway.

'If you can persuade the old git to let you stay over Thursday it should be no prob,' said Clare, slapping another strip of paste-soaked newspaper on to Erica's torso, bare except for the clingfilm in which it was wrapped.

'It always depends on his mood.' Erica was doing the same thing to her friend. At Tundra's suggestion they'd shot a roll of film of each other, walking, running, shouting, laughing. Longshots, close-ups. Photocopies of the pictures would then be cut-outs pasted over the torsos which, after the nipples had been painted silver, would rest on a framed bed of acrylic hair dyed the same colour as their own.

'Is there no way to sweeten him?' asked Clare.

'You're joking. Where would you begin with an orchard full of lemons? But I'm going to risk staying out. Gareth's more important to me than him losing his rag.'

'We'll try the dedicated student taken ill at her studies during the evening. I'll ring your folks, say you've been put to bed. Even he can hardly come and drag you out. Hold still.' Having decided the papier mache was of the required thickness Clare turned on the hairdryer to firm it. Then it would be peeled off and propped up to dry properly.

'Ow. Mind my tits, will you!' Erica jerked backwards and Clare lowered the heat, 'Clare, you do think that dress I found is all right? I mean, is it obvious it's someone's throw-out?'

'Not now you've washed it. It looks amazing on you. Think, girl. You've already managed to light his fire wearing old togs at the library. When he sees you in that he'll be microwaved. Put your arm up.'

Erica curled her toes in an anticipatory wriggle at the vision of next Thursday. She and Gareth were to make a foursome with Clare and Darrel, to go dancing at Razzlers, the club everyone in college talked about. She was hitting the town. At last.

CHAPTER EIGHT

Doris watched Alb cycle down the Close and safely disappear round the corner. He used his bike on fine days, or when he wasn't transporting items from work, in the interests of economy. She'd checked with Erica that this was a morning Tundra wouldn't be in college. Apparently her time was divided between teaching on three days a week and painting at home. Last night Doris was desperate to see her and lay awake till dawn, seized with a mad urge to rush round straight away. Fall to her knees to beg Tundra's aid.

Now she held back, nervous fingers touching the letter that had lain accusingly in her apron pocket since the arrival of yesterday's post. She paced the mat, straightened a tea towel, wiped a crumb. Taking a gasp of air, she plunged round to Number Seven.

In answer to her pounding Tundra materialized, majestic in a turban of towels secured by a kilt pin, a smeared smock flowing to her ankles.

'Morning, luvvy. Thanks for the flowers. Come in. I'm giving my head a soak in cooking oil as I work. To revive the follicles.'

'I'm sorry to trouble you when you're busy. But if you could spare ten minutes for something very important,' she was trembling.

'It's break time anyway.' Tundra dragged on her cigarette, 'been at it since six. I've a collection of my work to finish for an exhibition at the end of June. But I'm nearly there.' She stretched, gave a gusty sigh, and pointed into the dining room as they went past. Doris saw extra tables set up with unfinished paintings leaning on them. She knew nothing of art yet felt shapes, colours, all giving off the same potent energy as Tundra herself.

'So, why are you jittery?' Her shovel hand tilted Doris's chin as they waited for the kettle.

'Tundra, something terrible's happened. I feel - I can't talk to anyone about the mess I've made. You're the only person I can tell.'

'How flattering. Yes, I'm a safe repository of dark secrets. Heard some in my time, chuck.'

'I need advice. You see, it's Alb -' she trailed off.

'Right. What's he been up to?' Tundra's glance hardened.

'Nothing like - like that. He's a good man, you know.'

'Hmm. I can see and hear, Doris. I've talked to people since I came. I know plenty who aren't his fans.'

A tear splashed on the worktop. It was the first time she'd heard anyone outside the family criticise Alb. To realise he wasn't universally regarded as a paragon was a relief.

'I'm at my wits end. This arrived yesterday.'

Tundra took the letter, scanned it. With raised eyebrows she looked at Doris.

'Well, I wouldn't describe it as terrible if they wrote to say I'd won a car. Congratulations!'

'You don't understand. It's a prize from *Gossy*.

'*Gossy*? Oh, I know. That mag with salacious stories and household tips. I see it in waiting rooms.' Tundra chuckled.

'It'd be an exciting thing for a lot of people, but Alb will be livid if he finds out. He's forbidden me to read nearly all the women's magazines. He'll know I've been buying Gossy. That I've betrayed his trust. Life will be - difficult.'

For a moment Tundra's expression was inscrutable. From her session with Bernardine she'd picked up a lot about the workings of the Wakes family.

Doris said, 'I need to cover this up, somehow get rid of it without him knowing. Please, please will you help me? Will you tell Gossy I can't accept, I don't want my name and address printed amongst the winners?' She chewed her nails, 'or perhaps you would advise me how to sell it? Then if I give the money to the church roof fund it won't seem so bad when he hears.'

'No,' she rumbled angrily. Doris flinched.

With slow deliberation Tundra brewed tea, poured it out,

her brows creased. 'No, Doris. Come and sit down.' Her tone was milder.

Doris was marched into the front parlour, pressed onto the chaise longue. Leaning an arm on the mantlepiece Tundra re-read the letter.

'Taxed, insured, a year's free petrol. What you are going to do, my dear, is obvious. You are going to learn to drive.'

Doris gaped. A strong force seemed to have flattened her against the seat. 'What...? No! I can't. I could never do that.'

'I shall teach you myself.'

'It's impossible,' gasped Doris, 'Alb will never allow it.'

'Allow?' Tundra spat out in a shower of ash. She threw her fag end into the grate. 'He won't be told. Not until it's fait accompli. He won't see the car, or you learning. A very dear friend of mine lives by the rugby fields. He'd let us park it at his place. He's the discreet sort who won't tell anyone till you're ready.'

'I'd never be ready. I haven't the courage to get behind a wheel.' Doris was flabbergasted, 'Alb says the roads are plagued with madmen. He's right, you know. We've had many a near miss. And then, what if I knock someone down?'

'Everyone thinks like that at first. Listen, luvvy, people get killed in their living rooms. Planes fall out of the sky, walls collapse. We must all do our best and trust to fate. I taught my lads and they're excellent drivers.'

'I mean, what call would there be for me to learn?' Doris floundered, trying to extricate herself from this outlandish notion. 'Whenever we go out he drives.' She clutched at excuses. Tundra was almost as frightening as Alb himself in her insistence.

'Don't you occasionally go out on your own?'

'N-not really.'

'Then it's time you did. Driving will be a real asset to you.'

She began making plans about forms, a provisional

112

licence, as Doris sank back, lightheaded, wishing she hadn't mentioned it, unable to believe any of it. She decided it was an hallucination, and gulped the tea hopefully, as if it were some divine potion to turn the world right way up.

Bernardine felt Shaun's presence in every inch of Land o' Green. The leaves, the flowerpots, the bags of gravel, her whole body were permeated by the knowledge of him. Since Saturday she had come in earlier than usual to avoid meeting him in the staff room where they put their coats. She had spent this morning alone in a greenhouse, pricking out houseplant seedlings, which all looked at her with his smile. Later, as she advised a customer on container grown trees, he trundled past on top of a load of peat driven by another worker, giving her a cheerful wave.

She flushed shamefully. Everyone seemed to be looking, sneering. She knew they weren't. Put him out of your mind, she admonished herself with stern futility. Yet she wanted to go up to him. How could you deceive me into loving you when all along you've got a wife, kids? Stupid. How stupid. She had made the whole thing up for herself, wanting it to be like the romance in her books. An ending with him clasping her. So tight they could never be parted.

Tundra had been right when they'd talked about it. 'Maybe you need to get this in perspective. When you've not been close to men it's easy to give them virtues, love, make them into heroes. Why not suggest going for a friendly drink? Then find out the facts, all his shortcomings. Seeing him, warts and all, still won't make it easy, but easier to distance yourself from him.'

But how could she? Since the incident on Saturday, Bernardine's need for him had intensified, become an illness. And she'd never asked anyone to go for a drink with her. With him it was unthinkable. She thought of the pub where he'd sat with his wife.

As the day had turned very warm the boss asked her to

check on the watering. She was hosing down the outdoor displays when Shaun came up to her, leaving no chance of evasion.

'Bernardine. Hi.' He held a lunch bag, sounded uncertain. She muttered a reply, but continued what she was doing.

'Bernardine.' He was more insistent, 'Bernie.' It was what everyone in work called her. Friendly. Acceptable. Not like Bernard.

'Yes?' She couldn't face him.

'For some reason you keep on avoiding me.'

'No, I don't. I've been busy.'

'Come on, Bernie. Every time you see me you walk in the other direction. I want to know what I've done to offend you so I can put it right.'

Bitterness squeezed her. His gaze was pressure on an aching wound.

'It's nearly twelve. At least sit down with me a minute. Please?'

They went to the bench and he took a flask from the bag.

'Coffee?' He passed a plastic cup and, as sun glinted on the liquid, remarked, 'the machine stuff's horrible. It always tastes nicer brought from home.'

Home immediately accessed an image of him with the dark haired woman. Bernardine's hand shook. After a flash of ice a huge nettle of pain gripped it as the hot water spilled. She howled in anguish.

'Quick!' He pulled her over to a tap, thrust the hand under it. 'Cold, running water. For at least three minutes.'

She was sobbing with pain. He stood behind, his arms round her. The mesh of golden hairs on them, his earthy scent, pierced her.

'There, Bernie.' Still holding her he walked her to the centre office where Mr Gray wrapped the hand in a dressing. He and Shaun tried to persuade her to go to casualty but she refused. Shaun could not be spared but the old man insisted on running her home immediately and ordered her to take the next day off.

'But I can't. We're so busy with Easter.'

'We'll manage.' At the house he urged her mother to make her see a doctor. Bernardine insisted she would go if it was no better by the next day. If it had improved she'd be in work. He took out a ticket for a big gardening exhibition on in town. 'You need a break from work. If you must do something take yourself to see that, gather me some brochures. If there's time I might drop in myself.'

Doris was disconcerted, as much by Bernardine's still dripping tears as by the injury. She hadn't seen her daughter cry since she was a child. She tried to comfort her but Bernardine would not allow it. Reverting, after a while, to her usual non-committal manner, she went up to her room. Her hand pulsated but she needed the pain to distract her. She lay reading for the next few hours, nursing her hurt, trying to lose herself in a kinder place.

Later on Tundra called and was told of the mishap.

'Leek juice, of course.' She brought the vegetables from her kitchen, sliced them, pounded them to a pulp. Brooking no refusal she unwrapped Bernardine's bandage and painted the liquid on the injury. Bernardine stared.

'It's stopped throbbing.'

'Of course it has, my chuck. Leeks are a neuralgic painkiller. Now the reflexology. Off with the socks.'

Her feet enclosed in Tundra's mighty palms Bernardine drifted to sleep. After a while the other two women went downstairs and Doris closed the door in case their conversation was heard from the living room. Tundra had brought the application form for a provisional licence, got the insurance adjusted so she could drive the car and squared things with the *Gossy* office. There was to be no publicity, she told them, as the winner, like so many of their readers, lived in fear of an abusive partner who would cause trouble. Doris thought it sounded awful, put like that, as if Alb was completely unreasonable. 'Don't be daft. He is.'

Casey reminded her.

'I can't spare the time to pick her up today so we'll do it first thing tomorrow,' said Tundra. 'And bring some identification. Receipts, gas bills something like that with your name on.'

'They all have Alb's on. I, er, don't handle money much.'

'Passport then?'

Doris shook her head, 'we've never been abroad.'

'You do have a marriage certificate? A National Health number?'

Doris, concious of the clock, was relieved when she didn't stay. It would be too embarrassing to explain that Alb had decreed her persona non grata in Number Nine. She knew Tundra had drawn her onto dangerous ground. But, no, she admitted to herself it wasn't against her will. She was scared stiff yet excited by agreeing to something so daring, something Alb would never let her do.

He was extremely put out that Bernardine's scalded hand meant she couldn't join them at the hall that evening.

'I hope you realise you've put us behind schedule. You two will have to work harder to make it up.' He frowned at Erica and Harriet. Harriet wondered if there would ever be a time when she could please herself. Erica worried that he might make it a reason to stop her going to Clare's on Thursday and began to devise a strategy.

CHAPTER NINE

As they were rollering the walls the vicar looked in. He shone with the glow of one stepping from a hot bath. He had the habit of shifting from foot to foot when gripped by enthusiasm and now almost tap-danced across the hall.

'Wait till you hear my tremendous news. Something absolutely marvelous.'

Alb put on his community expression and the girls also paused to listen. 'Don't stop,' Alb ordered, as if they were children, 'get on with it while I speak to Mr Coulson.'

'You remember Mrs Goodwin, who died recently?' said the vicar.

'Ah yes. I installed a hand rail so the poor soul could get up her front step,' nodded Alb. 'It wrung your heart to see the way she struggled on her pension. Denied herself everything to spend it all on those cats.'

'That's it, Alb. She was far from struggling. When her husband died she inherited shares but never used the dividends. It seems she was saving them for a rainy day. They grew into a small fortune which she's willed to St. Chad's.'

Now they all suspended painting to stare.

'The bulk will be used in our overseas mission work, the water projects in Africa. Quite right of course. And some for church renovation and parish schemes.'

'Wonderful.' Alb agreed faintly. He tried to equate the idea of wealth with Mrs Goodwin's house that always smelt of mould and cats' urine, its cupboards filled with tins of Whiskas, the beans she ate on toast made with the cheapest of white loaves. He thought of the 1970s coat she wore to church.

'The dear lady was not only a lifelong parishioner of St. Chads,' the vicar went on, 'but it appears she and her husband were leading lights of our dramatic society in the fifties. I've been told there was a thriving one in those days.'

'It was still active up to five years ago,' said Alb, 'but petered out due to lack of support. It's a shame.'

'Well, I'd already decided to revive it. Now we'll do it in style. Mrs Goodwin's made a special bequest to be spent on equipping St. Chad's drama group.'

He sat on the edge of the stage, bubbling with plans. The hall would make an ideal little theatre. Of course it would need to be modified, extra dressing room space built on, a lighting box constructed. He knew of a theatre that was closing, the seating was practically going begging. It folded back on platforms so could be rolled out of the way when they needed the hall for other use.

'Of course we'll buy our sound and lighting rigs brand new. State of the art equipment. You know I acted before I got my Calling? My old drama tutor's an expert in the field and will give us advice.'

Alb listened, feeling control of the hall, his hall as he thought of it, moving away from him. Mr Coulson saw he was trying to look keen.

'You realise I'll rely on your input for this project, Albert? We'll need someone reliable. Someone competent to deal with the technical side.'

Alb's dour features brightened, 'you can count on me, Jeff.' The pencil line of his mouth curved to a smirk. He saw himself taking a curtain call. A round of applause. The picture in the paper, 'Brilliant Stage Manager Saved Our Show, Say Cast.'

Harriet's ears had pricked up. They'd need someone to do the costumes. She longed to mention to the vicar that she'd helped design sets for a couple of Spraffy's clients, but thought better of it. If she asked openly to join the drama group her father would find a way to block it. As part of the company she might make or do something to draw praise and, in the Wakes family, that must belong exclusively to him. Still, she intended having a word in private with Mr Coulson.

The following morning Bernardine didn't wake until seven when she rolled over as Erica shook her.

'Happy Birthday, Bernie!' Her sisters and mother were thrusting cards at her. She blinked, having genuinely forgotten.

'I persuaded Dad to let you sleep in this once as it's your birthday and because of your hand. How is it, love?'

'Much better.' She sat up, looked at the cards, unwrapped the packages with her left hand. Tights, socks, soap. From Erica an enamel brooch shaped like a pansy. The message in the card from her parents was 'Love from Mum and Dad' in Doris's handwriting.

When the others had gone to work Doris told her she was going over to give Mrs Tyler a hand with something. She knew Bernardine wouldn't tell Alb. None of them told him anything.

Bernardine took the bus into town. The shock of the accident had triggered a defiance in her that she had never known. When she got up she left her hair unbunned, put on the clothes so long dormant in her tallboy, pinned the little brooch to her sweater. Twenty-four seemed old to her. Never to have had contact with men, then, so suddenly, for this one to trigger a volcano of hurting, wanting, was a cruel awakening.

From the top deck she watched passers by. So many lovers. Mostly teenagers, holding hands as they stepped their intoxicating dance through the streets, tasted each other at intervals. A black girl walked past in lime green coat and shoes, beads swinging in her braids, the very spirit of spring, heading somewhere special, to a waiting someone. As the bus passed Alexandra Park Bernardine glimpsed the lake shimmering through the trees. Even the swans were swimming in pairs.

She alighted, her spirits dragging to the pavement as she moved through sunshine. At the exhibition centre she waited while her name tag was tapped out then trudged round the temporary village of stalls.

The aisles were crammed with endless arrays of gardening aids, miracle manures, greenhouse heaters. Every time she stopped to look she was accosted by people in smart suits, wielding clipboards. They kept turning into Shauns then back into strangers.

The exhibition hall had been converted from a main-line railway station. The high airiness of its roof span lit a Shaun in every corner, walking away, walking towards her in his familiar jeans and brown leather jacket. She would hurry after him, about to speak his name then he would turn into someone else. As she stared listlessly at motor mowers another one approached her.

It was him.

'Morning, Bernie. How is it?' Delicately he touched a finger to her bandage.

She swallowed several times, had to wait for the thunderous hammering of her heart to subside.

'Still twingeing slightly. Getting back to normal.' She examined her dressing as if it was the most riveting item in the hall, 'I thought Mr Gray was coming.'

'He got involved with invoices. He wanted me to check you as well as the exhibition. I must be back this afternoon.'

Her flush was replaced by disappointment. He was here because the boss had sent him. What a fool she was. He gestured towards the stalls, 'I'm saturated with all this. What about you?'

'Yes,' she held up a stack of information packs, 'it's all here in any case.'

They fell silent as people milled round them. Someone pushed her against him.

'Could you use a cool drink, Bernie? Not here though. I know a nice place we could have lunch.'

'Okay.' Even though he hadn't chosen to be with her there was a hurtful pleasure in walking beside him down the street.

In the canal-side pub she ordered lager. She wasn't

hungry but nodded when he suggested a ploughman's. She sat at one of the tables in the yard, listening to a guitarist playing on the raised stage against one wall. Shaun returned with a loaded tray.

'Please don't think I'm stingy but I bought one we can share.'

Bernardine stared at the monster French loaf on its bed of salad and pickles.

'Gosh. There's at least half a pound of cheese in it.'

'They're famous for their massive butties. I've known one feed up to four people. There's a rumour the place is owned by Desperate Dan.'

'It's lovely.' She looked round at the tubs of flowers, the nearby lock-keeper's cottage reflecting in the water.

'Since they trendied up the old warehouses into flats it's got more popular. Today it's peaceful but at the weekend it'll be heaving. It's the annual narrow boat rally.' He looked at her, 'ever been?' She shook her head. 'They have a market. And a great programme of street theatre. I'm going to bring my kids. It's my turn to have them.'

Light, warmth, music flooded through Bernardine. She was emboldened to say, 'I saw them with your wife last week.'

'Ex. Laura's my ex.' As he confirmed it the full Hallé orchestra swelled her heart. 'We've been divorced two years. She lives with her new partner.' He paused a moment, looked away. 'They're having a kid in the autumn. We all keep it amicable for the boys' sake. I have them every other weekend. Sometimes babysit during the week.'

They ate in silence as she absorbed this information. He felt in his jacket, passed her an envelope, 'from the boss.'

Touched, she opened the card. 'That's thoughtful of him. He remembers all the staff birthdays.'

'Lucky he mentioned it or I wouldn't have known. This one's from me.' He leaned across and kissed her cheek, making her blush, 'Happy Birthday, Bernie.'

Another card and a small box. Self conscious, delighted,

she opened it, stared at the earrings. Unbelievable. A man, the man, had given her a present. It must be his own idea. The boss wouldn't have told him to buy her a present. For several seconds she was unable to speak.

'They are all right? I wasn't sure -'

'Shaun they're lovely.'

'Are you going to try them on?'

'I would,' she hesitated, 'except they're for pierced ears.' She saw his disappointment, 'but I've always meant to get them done and now I have a reason.'

'I must go soon. Bernie. I was wondering, d'you fancy joining us here on Sunday? I checked it's your day off.'

She thought of the church hall, Sunday at Number Nine, her father shouting, her mother upset. She thought of Shaun's hairy arms.

'Yes,' she answered. 'What time?'

They strolled back to where he had parked. Declining his offer of a lift back to Riffton she headed into the city centre and went to a jewelers that offered ear piercing.

'If you would sign here, madam. And then here.' The salesman handed his pen to Doris. The motor sale room authorized by *Gossy* was a vast box filled with gleaming models which, behind glass, appeared remote as sculptures in a gallery, unconnected to the smoking melee outside.

'This way,' he led the two women out to a yard filled with new cars. 'This one's yours, Mrs Wakes.'

'Oh,' said Doris, 'Oh, Tundra.'

'She is a little beauty,' Tundra patted the roof of the red car. 'In you get then.' The man offered to drive them around the block but Tundra had driven that model before. She thanked him, took the key but didn't start the engine right away, watching her friend with amusement.

Doris was stroking the windows, the wheel, the dashboard, inhaling the newness of the upholstery. It's mine, she thought. This marvelous thing actually belongs to me, Doris Wakes, car owner. And all for solving a puzzle.

It was strangely comfortable being driven by Tundra who moved the driver's seat back to accommodate her legs. Her bulk still filled the space, her head almost brushing the ceiling. When driven by Alb, Doris was always nervous, expecting disaster. It was far more agreeable to surrender her will to Tundra than to him. As they swept along Doris still didn't believe that at any point in the proceedings she herself would drive. She had agreed with everything Tundra had planned for her whilst recognising the impossibility of it. How could she, a woman incapable of doing her own shopping, be in charge of this large, lethal lump of metal? For the moment she would enjoy the outing and when asked would have a go. It would become obvious how useless she was, not to be trusted with so dangerous an object. Then Tundra would agree that it should be disposed of. A thought occurred to her. Maybe she could give it to Tundra.

It was as if the two of them were sitting side by side on a couch. Her neighbour seemed to have the measure of other road users without any desire to scream insults at them from the privacy of the car, or overtake just to be in front at the lights. As the scenery scrolled past at a steady pace Doris admired the way she wove through the traffic which was becoming heavier as midday approached.

'She goes sweet as a bird,' said Tundra, 'but we'll get away from this clag-up and give her a proper spin.' She negotiated several traffic jams, took short cuts up side streets, and within half an hour they were in countryside. Vistas of fields, trees, the occasional farmhouse. She turned down a bumpy lane and into a flat field stretching to some derelict buildings in the distance.

'What is this place?' Doris kept silent when she was in the van with Alb. Now she could ask questions without fear of ridicule.

'A disused airfield. It's been out of commission a long time but now it's owned by one of my old pupils who gave up art and became an entrepreneur. He's bought it to develop but you can use it. You're not allowed on the road before your Provisional comes, y'see, but you're okay on private land.'

'Use it? But I,...but...' Fear gripped her.

Tundra stopped the car and turned to give her a kindly appraisal.

'It's why we're here, lass. Look,' she indicated the view. 'Not a house, vehicle or pedestrian in sight. Not even a chicken for you to knock down. Okay, change places.'

'Now...?'

'Right now,' said Casey from the back seat. Doris took a deep breath.

Doris, a bit wobbly, did as she was told. Methodically, quietly, Tundra explained the controls. 'Now, turn on the ignition.'

Heart bumping, Doris did so and the engine purred.

'I can't -'

'Take your time. You can do it.'

'Of course you can!' snapped the voice from the back seat. Doris sat up straight. 'Stop this wimpish behaviour and get on with it.' Casey melted through the back of the seat into Doris's body. She put her hands on the wheel.

'This is neutral,' said Tundra. 'Take her into first. That's it. Foot up gently.'

They moved forward. Doris's mouth was dry but Tundra calmly talked her to the end of the runway, where she did a U-turn and came back. There was some kangaroo jumping, gear-grinding, a swerve on to the grass. But, after more tries Doris was gliding up and down the stretch of concrete. It was magic. You swung her wheel and the little darling obeyed. You put your foot down and she was off.

Casey took over. Her hands turned the wheel, her feet played the pedals. The car zoomed forward and sped down the runway, the speedometer swam up to forty, fifty, sixty.

'Yippee!' Doris heard Casey yelling out of her mouth.

'Slow down now. Now! Into third. Now second.' Tundra's

voice was urgent as they approached the end of the concrete, 'turn. Turn the wheel!'

With a squeal of rubber the car swung round and Doris sent it whizzing back. She felt Casey's foot through hers, pressing on the accelerator.

'Luvvy! Luvvy! Take it easy. Remember you must watch the speedo when you do it for real.' Tundra's eyes had widened.

'Ooh, sorry,' she braked jerkily, turned to her friend, 'isn't it marvelous? I drove her.'

'Of course you did,' said Tundra.

'Like I said you would,' added Casey, then disappeared.

Tundra leaned back, exposing her fence of teeth, 'well, Doris, you're hooked. Of course it's a bit trickier once you get out there but it'll come with practice. It's time we got back.'

Checking her watch Doris was astonished to see they had been there more than an hour. They drove back to Riffton where Tundra parked in the driveway of her friend's house, picked up her own car and returned them to Turvey Close. After thanking her Doris went in to Number Nine to cook the evening meal. Her hair, her nerves, her spirits all seemed to stand on end with exhilaration. She was lightheaded with joy.

'Amen,' the family murmured. Alb untwined his hands and looked across the table. What had Doris reminded him to do? Wish Bernard a happy birthday.

'Bernard,' he began, 'many - ' He stopped as, very deliberately, Bernardine pushed back her hair and revealed the gold studs in her ears.

'Wow, you've - ' Erica checked herself. Glanced at her father.

'My God. What do you think you've done to yourself, lad? Look at him, Doris, like one of those freaks you see walking round.' His voice rose on a splutter of anger, 'what's brought this on? Trying to be trendy, are you? Trying to make your boring, useless self interesting? You're pathetic. That's what you are, pathetic.'

Doris herself was surprised but, as usual, made no reply to his rhetoric and continued to serve chips. Bernardine's sisters looked intently at her. I'm going to get mine done, Erica promised herself.

'It's disgusting. It's like those tags they put on things to stop shoplifters. D'you see me and your mother walking round with bits of metal stuck in us? And how much money did you waste getting mutilated?'

Bernardine said nothing but took her plate and cutlery, got up and left the room. Alb followed her into the hall, shouted to her to come back as she retreated upstairs. On the landing she turned an expressionless face to him. She raised the plate higher and higher in a Statue Of Liberty stance. He thought she wouldn't dare but, as the plate began to tilt, Alb swooped back into the kitchen in time to avoid being hit by a flying turkey burger and the rain of chips that threatened his authority. He returned to the table snarling, 'he's obviously unhinged. It's best if we ignore him till he snaps out of it.'

CHAPTER TEN

Doris was filled with a longing to drive again but there was no possibility until the following week when the college would be on holiday. Tundra had gone in today to see where her students were up to with projects, and also mentioned that both her sons would be home and there were friends dropping in for Easter.

At breakfast Alb announced he wouldn't be there to supervise work on the church hall that evening. The vicar had invited him on a visit to another parish to see the new sound and lighting rig they'd installed for their theatre group. He paused to smirk and put forward his ideas. The other vicar was trying to locate Jeff Coulson's old drama teacher who would be advising them. Listening to him, Harriet ached to go with them.

He gave his instructions to herself and Bernardine. They were to topcoat all the doors. Clean all brushes. Make sure all ladders were locked away. Turn off all lights. Secure all locks of the hall when they left.

'I can't paint with this,' Bernardine held up her bandaged hand.

'Wear a glove and use it to help your left one along.'

Erica was alarmed, 'anything for an upset stomach, Mum?' she asked, setting the scene for tonight, 'and I've a headache too.'

'If you feel ill you shouldn't go in, love. It is the last day of term.'

'No, it'll go away. I'll be all right,' she replied quickly, with a look of suffering kept nobly under control, 'I really, really want to finish this assignment tonight. It's a projected database for the running of a third world orphanage. If it's good enough they might actually use it.' On that note she grabbed her college bag and left before Alb could question her.

Most days Doris went out for a walk. Not having money she didn't approach the shops except on Fridays, when she got the fruit, veg and *Gossy*. Window shopping other times held no appeal as she was liable to bump into Mrs Copeland or one of her cohorts. As the standard of spotlessness at Number Nine was so high, and Alb had drilled everyone to army standards of tidiness, the house was easy to maintain and there were long, empty hours.

Today she changed her usual route and went towards the address where Tundra had parked the car. They had exchanged pleasantries with Tundra's friend, but, alarmed, Doris recognised him as Mr McCloud the manager of the building society Alb used. Tundra assured her his lips were sealed but Doris was glad he'd be at work now. She wanted to stand by herself and gaze.

It was a corner house with the drive paved in a large triangle. Behind a parked Land Rover and a boat on a trailer she saw the shiny red of her car. She couldn't summon the courage to go in, but stood on tiptoe, longing to stroke her as she had done yesterday. My little Rosie. Well, she wasn't being that stupid. Tundra had said 'she'. My little miracle. Me, driving you. Of her girls only Erica had mentioned learning to drive, a notion Alb had quickly quashed on the grounds of cost and natural incompetence. Doris had the happy thought that if she could do it she'd be able to teach Erica.

'Go on, you divvy,' hissed Casey in her ear, 'she does belong to you, y'know.'

Doris slipped through the gate. Tundra had the key so there would be no chance of Alb finding it, so Doris was unable to open the car. But she walked round, peering in, running her hands over the bodywork. She leaned her face against the roof, closed her eyes. Even the mere memory of that drive on the airfield gave her a thrill.

The woman next door came into her garden and, her back to Doris, began hanging out washing. Doris moved quickly into the road. But she glanced back, feeling an inner tug. It was like abandoning a pet animal, something she'd never had and always wanted. She swung along reciting the Highway Code. Tundra had given her a copy, which she had started testing herself with and which was kept hidden in the *Gossy* case. She had voiced dread at the thought of the day Alb must be told. Tundra said, 'we'll cross that one when we come to it.'

At Clare's house that evening a shrill screamfest was in progress between her and her younger sister, regarding people who hogged bathrooms and used other people's stuff without asking. Kelly was fourteen but their mother had been nagged into letting her go to an alchohol-free Christian-run disco at a club in Piccadilly. The youth group organising it were picking her up in their minibus and she was to be dropped back at half past ten.

'Do you know the price of that mascara? Do you?' Clare snatched it off her.

'At least let me finish. I've only done one side. Mean cow!'

Erica was also annoyed with Kelly. She wanted her friend's undivided attention to help her get ready for this date. If they didn't get a move on the boys would be here. The effect on them of sudden, stunning beauty would be lost. She assessed herself in the cheval mirror. Washed and pressed the dress revealed its pedigree. As she turned, it stretched and floated over her at the same time, fluid, simple. Her long legs ended elegantly in Clare's strap shoes, her curls were a copper crown.

Clare joined her and they admired their reflections, Kelly having gone downstairs for a screech at her mother over spending money.

'I'm so yummy I could eat myself.' Clare said.

'I've decided that what I am,' said Erica, 'is, what's the word? Voluptuous. I'm totally voluptuous.'

'I thought that was a tactful way of saying fat. You aren't fat.'

'How about slim with fat bits in crucial places? Yeah, that's me.'

'Aren't we a pair of babes?' They turned this way and that.

'To die for.' Erica blew herself a kiss. They collapsed on each other in hysterics.

'Right,' said Clare, 'let's get some slap on.'

When the boys arrived to pick them up, Gareth's expression gave Erica the best feeling she'd ever had about herself. They went into town by bus, planning to taxi back late. The four of them chatted in their personal micro climate of C.K. on the top deck of the 85. Sitting next to Gareth, Erica kept catching her breath, both with his nearness and the excitement she felt, poised to plunge into that other, scintillating Manchester so long denied her.

First they went for a drink at the Station House. She'd visited the first floor café in daytime tameness. At night she knew its glacier walled bar was one of the places to be seen. Shifting on her chrome chair she arranged herself to best advantage then saw nobody appeared to notice anyone else. Everyone ignored the people around them, concentrating on the friends at their own tables as her own group did. At least Gareth couldn't stop looking at her. The two of them dissected the bar menu, devising another. After her second drink she was fed up with the place but Gareth persuaded her to share his beer. By the time they walked round the corner to Razzlers her veins held a convivial warmth. A queue slowly squeezed its way in as bored doormen waved them past.

'They're supposed to ask for I.D. but they never do,' murmured Clare. 'Loads of people here are under age. Not that we are. Not for much longer.'

As they stepped on the dance floor the soles of her feet pulsed as it vibrated with the movement of dozens of people. It was a proper sprung floor as the venue was officially Razzlers Ballroom, still the scene of occasional contests, a live band on regular nights. Tonight a D.J. was on stage, his voice blasting decimated words through the speakers 'Remix/new/blum/allbeenwaiting/blum/ release/last/groovin'/yeah!/blum/at number three/blum/ hear it!'

Everyone looked so good. Guys' sculpted or shaved heads, girls' flashing thighs and arms. Watching, Erica was intimidated and had to remind herself she was on a par with them, she could compete. Reticent at first, she started dancing with Gareth in the way she'd often practised in Clare's bedroom. But the place was so packed she stopped thinking everyone was thinking how clumsy she looked and began to enjoy it. The loudness of the music thrummed through her bones. It was like being underwater, unable to speak so they fishmouthed words to each other. With every number Erica's movements picked up more energy. The sound pumped through her, took hold of her. She didn't want to stop.

In one of the pauses she found herself soaked in sweat. Together their party came off the floor and went to the balcony that ran round the room. Gareth brought refreshments from the bar and they cooled off, watching the flickering mass below, picking out people they recognised from college.

'It's always packed in the holidays,' said Clare. 'Mind our drinks,' she ordered the boys, 'we won't be long.'

Following her through a door backstage, Erica recognised the same leafy aroma of roll-ups they'd tried privately at Clare's. They went along a passage which appeared to stretch the length of the building, passing small gaggles of smokers who stood talking. Some danced in a style and were dressed in clothes that seemed quaint, hippyish compared to those in the main ballroom.

There was another queue outside the toilets at the end. In the Ladies it was impossible to freshen their make-up for a crush of girls leaning on washbasins to reach the mirrors, nearly eating their reflections.

'Like it?' asked Clare, mopping her face with a tissue.

'Brilliant. My first proper date with Gareth. No horrible mates or sudden grandmas.' They giggled. Clare had heard about the onion soup debacle.

Refreshed, they went back and danced again. In the whirl of lights Gareth held her, kissed her, let go, held her, their clothes swampish in the damp heat. The movement from the floor throbbed up her legs, made her insides reverberate. She was aware of sweat dripping off her as a piercing wave of desire took hold when she felt Gareth pressed close against her stomach. Excited, she realised he was also affected. They clasped each other, locked by the numbing beat, by the hothouse atmosphere. She felt she was being liquidised by aliens. Fantastic, her melting brain told her. Bliss. Wanna die. Die now. Total Paradise. Yeah!

'Shit! Shit! Shit!' It was Clare's angry voice in her ear.

'What?' Grumpy at being disturbed, trying to unglaze their eyes, they tried yelling over the music.

'Over there. Look,' mimed Clare, pointing.

It was difficult trying to pick out individuals in the bobbing, heaving, constantly highlighted mass.

'There,' mouthed Clare, taking Erica's arm. 'It's Kelly and her mate.' Darrel and Gareth bent to catch the gist of what she was saying. 'My kid sister's over there and she's drunk.'

They pushed through the press of people but the younger girls kept weaving ahead of them so they couldn't catch up. Eventually the posse led by Clare managed to corner them. Kelly's legs anglepoised against the wall as her mate tried to hold her up. They were talking to a young man who had homed in on Kelly, who was giggling at him, twining her arm round his neck. Clare turned an outraged face to her friends, snarled, then launched herself at him.

'Hey, you, get away from her! Now!' Clare pounced, dragging at him so he staggered.

'What's your problem?' He turned aggressively, went to

132

push her. On seeing the size of her male escorts he backed off but threw her an angry glance before disappearing into the crowd.

'I know that guy,' she said, 'he deals. Sells the kids Whizz, and the rest. Scabby bastard.'

'Gerroff,' slurred Kelly, shaking a disheveled head as her sister grabbed her. 'Whycancha livme lone?'

'We need to get her out or there'll be trouble if she's seen like this. Take her other arm, Erica.'

With an ill grace they manhandled a sniggering Kelly into the fresh air. Slung between them she lurched with rubbery movements, followed by her friend. Clare began to scold the other girl who maintained it was Kelly's fault for getting them thrown out of the church club. Kelly had smuggled in a whiskey bottle jammed down her pants. They'd had a drink in the loo.

'I only took a couple of swigs. She drank the rest then fell downstairs. That was when they knew. They ordered a taxi to take us home but while we were waiting in the doorway we legged it.'

'I'm sorry,' Clare frowned to her friends, 'but I can't leave the silly little cow to get in more hassle. I'll ring the club so they know she's not murdered, then find a taxi. There's no reason why you three can't go back to Razzlers.'

No, they assured her, she needed help. Together they walked Kelly round Piccadilly Gardens to sober her up. She staggered down the path, shook off her sister and collapsed on a seat. 'Wanna cig?' she asked the pungent tramp sitting by her. Taking out a box of matches she struck one, held up her finger, then looked puzzled, focusing with difficulty as she tried to set light to it.

'Come on, Kelly.' Erica drew her to her feet. Kelly broke into sobs then threw up spectacularly over her. A bomb in a soup factory.

At St. Chad's Harriet and Bernardine were taking a

breather. Even with the glove, Bernardine's hand was painful when it touched anything. She wished she'd been able to tell her father she wasn't going to come here. But she couldn't, and despised herself. Although Shaun's gift engendered an initial rush of courage and she looked forward to their date on Sunday, doubts had crept in. She knew he was now the most important thing in her life. Yet she struggled against herself, trying to damp down the emotion that possessed her.

There were no guarantees when it came to men, she warned herself. She'd learned that much from countless overheard conversations between Tina and Sue. Time and again she witnessed one or the other coming in to work starry eyed over some man. Definitely 'the one' for a few months, once even for a year, until things inevitably fell apart. The women comforted each other with bitter humour every time it happened. Yet they continued searching for the ideal lover, out there somewhere, a bloke who would treat them properly.

Tina's last boyfriend was in a similar situation to Shaun. Bernardine heard her complain about the attachment he had for his kids and that she suspected he still had strong feelings for his ex-wife. Bernardine wondered if that could be the case with Shaun.

Absently Bernardine swished a brush clean in a jar of turps. She began to feel depressed. Maybe he had come on to her because she was a safe bet, not likely to go off with anyone else. Because who else would want her?

'You look down in the dumps,' said Harriet.

'I've had enough of this.' Bernardine threw the glove on the floor.

'Me too.' Harriet was more aggrieved than usual at missing a show. She'd put a lot of herself into those *West Side Story* costumes. Now she was slogging here while he went swanning off, talking theatre. She stood up, 'I've got an idea.'

She fetched empty containers, bean cans, coffee jars,

from the bin outside the hall kitchen. Picking up a paint tin she tipped the contents into them, stuffed them with paper towels to stop leakage. Bernardine helped until all the paint was gone. Then they hid them in the trash, standing them upright so they'd set hard. They shared a grin over the totally uncharacteristic act.

'There. We're out of paint so we can't continue. Home, eh?' They nodded. Neither of them ever talked much to each other yet Harriet itched with curiosity as to why Bernardine had got her ears pierced. At last she asked, 'do those hurt?'

'No. But you must keep the studs in for six weeks till they heal. You turn them each night with a dab of the antiseptic they give you. After that you can wear any style.'

Harriet wanted to ask her more but thought better of it. If Bernie was starting to think about her appearance it was an opportunity for her sister to advise and dress her.

When they got back, Doris was watching a permitted wildlife programme. On screen mating baboons were screeching but, in Alb's absence, she hadn't bothered with the egg-timer and continued to knit. Bernardine changed out of overalls and said she was going to the phone box, something she rarely did. Nobody asked why she didn't use the hall phone.

Harriet gave a sigh of contentment. There was still a good chunk of the evening left. In her bedroom she took the cover off her sewing machine, got out a box of assorted materials and pulled aside the tiny curtain that hid her best girl, Tartine Zircon.

Tartine was not a Barbie, Cindy or any of the bootleg teendoll models adorning the walls. She was almost twice as large as they with a more adult face and body. Harriet had found her in a boot sale, battered and dusty, wearing some indeterminate national costume. Even in that state Harriet had recognised her compelling glamour. Twenty five of the teendolls were black but it wasn't clear if Tartine was supposed to be black, white or mixed race. She had the rich apricot tone of a sunbed addict but could have been Spanish or South American. She had a sensual red mouth, brown eyes that were set-in, not painted on, black brows, lashes and curly hair.

She stood apart in a special niche that Harriet had made her, a kind of open-fronted cupboard with a pediment and pinnacles, like the shrine of some eastern household god, hung above the bedroom door.

Harriet took her down, testing scraps of silk against her. She began her usual dialogue, an ongoing serial of Tartine's adventures, usually carried on between Harriet and Ann taking different roles. In her friend's absence she addressed the doll directly.

'So we'll make you a midnight blue gown for the ambassador's ball. But be careful because he knows about his rival and -'

There was a ring at the doorbell. Harriet heard Tundra booming to her mother. Next minute Doris called to her and Harriet reluctantly came down.

'Do you know the name of that plumber, love, the one your Dad's friends with? Tundra has a problem.'

'The bloomin' loo won't work,' said Tundra, 'I've fiddled with it but I'm so cack-handed with anything the least technical. Got to get it sorted as I've a house-full this weekend.'

'If Alb wasn't out he'd mend it for you, I'm sure.' Doris wasn't at all sure, in view of his ravings about the Tylers. She gave Harriet a glance of supplication.

'I'll get tools in case they're needed then come and have a look.' Harriet reassured them. She went out to the garage and Tundra turned to Doris.

'I'm afraid I'm useless too,' explained Doris, 'but he's brought them all up as handymen.' She thought how strange that sounded.

It was the first time Harriet had been in Number Seven

since the Tylers moved in. Although it was the same layout in reverse of the Wakes house it was so different. The chintzy presence of old Mrs Trevis was erased, replaced by a more exciting look. Underfoot there was sisal carpeting, oriental rugs and masks hung on white walls, a giant metal figure with outstretched wings stood on the landing.

In the bathroom she took the lid off the cistern, saw the hook that held the arm had come out and reconnected it. She pressed the handle and the lavatory flushed. 'There you go.'

'Thanks, chuck. You must stay and have a drink. A drop of wine?'

The front door banged. Someone came crashing into the hall.

'Germayn?' His mother leaned over the bannisters. He didn't reply but swerved into the front room, Tundra ran downstairs with a sound of sliding rubble, closely followed by Harriet.

He had his back to them, pouring himself a whiskey from the drinks table. They gasped as he turned round.

'Oh my Lord, who did that to you?'

There was a cut on his swelling lip, blood running from his nose, a vicious bruise round one eye. The sequinned dress he wore was ripped from armpit to knee, the maribou feather trim round hem and neck hanging in shreds. He looked like an exotic chicken savaged by a fox.

Tundra brought the First Aid box and tenderly administered to him. Harriet assisted with a damp facecloth and ice cubes to take down the swellings.

'Tell us what happened, my darling. Was it yobs again?'

'No, Mumzo. It was that bitch Candy. You know I told you the director devised a terrific new finale but wasn't sure who he wanted to star in it? I mean, it was fair and square that everyone had to audition again, just for that spot. I could see she was ravin' jealous when he decided it was me. She kept getting in sly digs. But this evening we were having a Dress and Tec rehearsal for the eleven o'clock

137

show.'

Harriet listened, open mouthed at the images this conjured. He went on, 'she just lost it. Said I'd been shagging Nathan so he'd choose me. She clouted me with a top hat so I hit her with me marble beads. Self defence. She went berserk and attacked me. Trashed the dressing room. Got her marching orders off Nathan, I can tell you.'

'I should think so. But what about you, love?'

'They all witnessed it, told him I wasn't to blame. I mean, he didn't sack me but could I go on like this? I took a taxi straight home. Now he'll have to cancel my spot. Worse, put one of the others in it.'

Harriet had exchanged greetings with Germayn in the street but not really spoken to him. She saw a few transvestites around Riffton, everyone knew the man from the curtain shop was one. Measuring out nets he was plain Mr Coker, but on his days off he and his wife looked like two middle aged sisters out shopping in matching cardigans and pearls. But occasionally, at things like the Mardi Gras carnival, she glimpsed dazzling glamour queens like Germayn. He was the first she'd studied close up, and even in his bedraggled condition she found him a strange, fascinating being.

'Are you too upset to do your act?' she asked.

'Well, no. I'd like to show 'em. But look at the state of me. This is an original.' Ruefully he lifted a flap of the dress, let it fall.

Harriet became suddenly brisk, 'take it off and I'll try to repair it on my machine. If you can disguise that with make-up,' she indicated his face, 'I've thought of something we can do about the eye. Ring your director and say you'll be there.'

They looked bemused. Then Tundra agreed, 'do as she says. She's a clever lass.'

Harriet went like the clappers, rooting through drawers, grabbing things, comparing, discarding. She closed up the seam so fast the machine seemed about to take off. Half an hour later she was back next door.

Germayn's slim figure towered next to his mother's massive one as she and Harriet got him back in the costume. The battered maribou sections had been removed, replaced by lengths of feather boa. His black eye was ripening horribly though.

'Here. Try this on.' From a carrier bag Harriet took a silver mask which, *Phantom Of The Opera* style, covered that side of his face. 'You'll get away with it. Just use a darker lippy so that cut on your mouth doesn't show.'

'I've got two fairy godmothers!' He looked relieved, 'I hope I can do it tonight.'

'We'll make sure you do. We'll come and give you moral support. What d'you say, Harriet?'

Harriet stared, felt a thrill. And resentment at Alb. By rights she should be at a show tonight.

'Give me a minute.'

She dived into Number Nine, grabbed a bag, gabbled an explanation to Doris and asked her to tell Alb, when he came in, that she'd gone to bed.

'I'll leave the spare back door key under the dustbin,' said her mother.

After her daughter had gone, Doris shivered with guilt. An avenging angel, looking a lot like Lily Wakes, hovered invisibly in the air, sword upraised over their sinful deceptions.

CHAPTER ELEVEN

The fragrance of daffodils and the voices of St. Chad's rather good choir filled the church on Easter Sunday. It had no effect on Alb who sat marinading in sourness. It was bad enough trying to get those half-witted lads to work properly when he wasn't around. They must have laid the paint on an inch thick to waste so much. He'd make them pay for it. Because of Easter he'd been in Tool Magic on Good Friday and the Saturday so couldn't supervise them. Then for this to happen!

On Thursday he began by enjoying the drive out with the vicar to view the other parish's drama set-up. It was in Wilmslow, a gilded stockbroker suburb, and Alb had a sense of his own importance as they turned in at the gates of the imposing vicarage.

'All Mr Hedley's friends welcome any excuse to visit him,' said Mr Coulson, 'his housekeeper lays on the most amazing teas.'

The said housekeeper let them in as the Reverend Hedley, his figure an endorsement of her cooking, welcomed them and was introduced to Alb. He led them to his study.

'I've a surprise for you, Jeff. I've tracked down your friend. Living in Riffton Hackets.'

'Riffton? That's incredible.'

As they followed him into the room Alb's smile vanished.

Tundra rose from the sofa, dwarfing them all, spreading her arms wide as the vicar ran into them.

'Jeff, lovey. How fabulous to see you after all this time!'

'And you, darling. I'd no idea you lived here. The last I heard you were in Sydney. I asked Hedley if he knew of an address where I could contact you and -'

He bubbled on excitedly. Tundra looked over his head, 'hello Albert.'

'You know each other? That small world syndrome

happens to me all the time.'

'He's my next door neighbour.'

'And my churchwarden.'

Alb felt there was some joke being perpetrated at his expense but couldn't fathom what it was.

'Of course I knew Alb and his family went to St. Chad's but not that was your patch, Jeff. I've not seen you since you were ordained.'

'This is so nice,' Mr Coulson beamed pinkly. 'It's true we're really one big family. Tundra's the person I mentioned, Alb, who tutored me on my drama course. We need your advice on sound and lighting, darling,' he said to her.

'Only too happy to show you what I know.' There was a sardonic glint in her expression as she looked at Alb, 'I enjoy teaching things to people'.

He seethed all through tea and the conducted tour of the hall afterwards. He had to listen to the vicar and Tundra reminisce about their past. It was a bad dream the way that woman sprang up and took over wherever he went. As they were leaving Mr Coulson said he hoped to see her in church at Easter.

'Definitely, darling. I've got both my boys and a house-full of guests for the holiday. We'll all come.'

Now Alb glared at four men sitting in the chancel, The Flex Tyler Quartet. The vicar had announced that St. Chad's was privileged to have such renowned international performers as guests at their worship. Well I'm not, thought Alb.

Tundra and Germayn, the latter wearing a dark eye patch but smartly suited, were in a pew behind him. Throughout each hymn he felt the smoky bass of Tundra's voice vibrate against his back. He suspected she was touching him up with the aid of sound to annoy him.

The musicians had already played an arrangement of *'Tis A Joy To Be Simple,* which was nothing like the tune he knew. After the next reading they launched into another number. As he heard the first, familiar bars he gripped the pew. *The Old Rugged Cross* was his all time favourite. To hear it murdered by that woman's son and his herd of perverts meant Alb could never again listen to his own copy.

As Flex sent the saxophone's voice to the roof angels, Erica was only half listening. Thoughts of Thursday night made her shudder. She stood on the pavement while Clare, profusely apologetic, tried to clean the mess off her with tissues. Kelly fell asleep in the taxi and snored all the way back to Clare's but Erica sat rigid with embarrassment, miserable in the knowledge she stank of puke. Bad enough if it had been her own, but to have someone else's ruin her date was the pits.

Yesterday had more than compensated. With her father safely at work she was free to drive into Cheshire with Gareth and the gourmet picnic he'd prepared to impress her. They had fun touring a stately home, pretending they were Lord and Lady Cobblers. Everything in it was theirs, the statues, the paintings, the heavily secured case of treasure including a bygone aristocrat's solid silver potty, a cause of much mirth.

A wander through the deer park put them in more romantic mood. In spite of crowds of visitors strolling about there were secluded areas to be alone. Mouth contact with the smoked salmon patties then with each other sent them into ecstatic melt down and they sank into the undergrowth. The sensations felt at Razzlers returned with a vengeance. They lay back, unzipping, caressing. As Gareth leaned over her Erica felt the trees above them spinning when he touched her. They were on a rollercoaster, travelling up, up to the top of the climb, about to whizz down to heaven. She squealed. Another face, covered in grey fur, peered through the ferns over his shoulder.

'Yah, shoo - go on!' They clapped and shouted. The buck,

scrounging for picnic scraps, turned and galloped off but the moment was lost. As they jumped up a group of people came past so they rearranged themselves and moved on.

In the evening there was an official invitation to tea at Gareth's Gran's. Erica saw a feisty little woman who adjusted her glasses to examine the visitor as they came in.

'My, she's right bonny and no mistake,' she told her grandson, instantly endearing herself to Erica, 'and what a redhead. Reminds me a bit of Rita Hayworth.' When they looked blank she explained, 'eeh, a real glamour girl she were in her day. A big film star in the Forties when me and your Great Aunty Joan were lasses. We tried to copy her. Chance would've bin a fine thing.' Her chuckle creaked round the kitchen.

When Gareth mentioned Erica's culinary ambitions it was the signal for an impromptu cookery session. His Gran hunted through cupboards for ingredients, fetched a loaf tin, greaseproof paper. She stood by, guiding Erica as she tried her hand at cake making.

'That's it, luv. Chop the dates small. You're supposed to soak 'em in cold tea overnight but we'll just give 'em half an hour while we're watching Cilla Black.'

Erica came away with a sense of achievement. Still no sex, she thought, but what a belting cake. She brought it home to share with her mother and sisters when Alb was out.

Harriet gave fervent thanks for her amazing evening at Saucy Girls. She had never been backstage in a professional theatre before and the atmosphere enchanted her. It appeared Tundra was known to the management and Harriet hovered in her shadow as she swept in, hugging, patting and teasing various people, giving wince-making slaps to the backsides of a couple of performers. There was a ribald badinage between them but Harriet detected an underlying respect she inspired in people.

Harriet looked round the dressing room, the costumes hung ready on the walls, the long, mirrored bench where Germayn and the others applied make-up. The bottles and jars. The exaggerated wigs on stands.

She'd brought a couple of plain eye patches for Germayn to wear in the chorus numbers. From the wings she took in the verve and precision with which he and the others danced. She often watched women dancers on television but now saw close up that men dressed as women moved with a different dynamic. Their bodies lacked a fluid judder that characterized the physique of even the fittest woman, imparting a feminine vulnerability. There was an immovable hardness to the Saucy Girls' figures. It reminded her of something. The teendolls. She noted that if she ever got to make costumes for these blokes she would go about it in the same way as when she sewed for her girls.

She and Tundra watched, rapt, as Germayn went into his solo routine. Later, as Tundra drove them home Harriet said with awe, 'you really can sing.'

'So they tell me. I take lessons when I can afford it. Mumzo coaches me a bit and I study films of old stars. It went off all right, didn't it? A big, big thank you, Harriet.' He gave her a theatrical kiss. It was a pleasing acknowledgement.

'But you could get much more out of your act,' she said earnestly. 'That bit where you come down the steps, you were too fast. You needed to slink down them. Look at the audience without a word, kind of weigh them up, y'know? Then you give a sigh - like this. And into the song.'

It was quiet in the car for a minute. Harriet was dismayed at having spoken out of turn, then Tundra said, 'yes. I see what she means. Yes. That would've made more impact. I suppose I'm too uncritical because I'm your mother. You should ask Harriet to help with your Dreamstars entry.'

'Dreamstars? On telly? Oh, I love that show. You're going in for it?' She sat up straight.

'I kept trying to get on but they're snowed under with applicants, thousands of em,' Germayn rested his chin on his hand. 'Again and again I tried, made it to the final auditions but not the heat. This time I've got through as a contestant on the next heat.'

'You're going to appear on television. Where? When?' Harriet clasped her hands.

'In town. In less than a month. I'm chuffed, of course. Millions watching me. And it's live.'

'I think that was the real cause of Candy's jealous outburst,' said Tundra. 'There's a lot of these talent contests and lookalike shows. Dreamstars is a bit different because it's for semi-professionals.'

'I've only got a few spots at Saucy's. I work part time at a health food shop in the gay village.'

'He gets my aromatherapy oils at cost.' Tundra put in.

'I mean,' Germayn went on, 'all my friends say how well I've done getting on Dreamstars. But it's not like Saucy's. I've been appearing in shows since I was a kid and I love playing to an audience. I mean, you're seeing them react, seeing their faces. But this is different. I'm terrified I'll mess it up. I almost wish I wasn't doing it.'

'You didn't tell me you felt that way,' Tundra patted him.

'The TV people believe in you. You must believe in yourself,' said Harriet. She took a deep breath. 'If you think I could be of any use I'd be only too pleased to work on it with you.' Her own boldness threw her.

She thought it wise to follow up with a few credentials and for the rest of the journey explained to them about her Spraffy's projects. They listened to her with respect, she noticed. They were seriously considering the idea. She was on such a high she never gave a thought to the Alb question until they turned into Turvey Close.

The vicar was giving the final blessing. As he made the Sign Of The Cross, Casey whispered to Doris, 'First, Second,

145

Third, Reverse,' and Doris almost gestured the gears. With a jolt she remembered where she was and beckoned to the girls for them to organise refreshments.

Passing out teas and coffees from the counter she didn't experience her usual tension, a readiness to fend off any barbs directed her way from Mrs Copeland and Co. It was due to Tundra's reassuring presence in the hall. After they exchanged a brief greeting her friend was surrounded by people wanting to talk to her, not least the vicar. The musicians were being congratulated, commiserations expressed to Germayn for his facial injuries caused when he was helping a friend cut down an overhanging branch. Tundra stood at the centre, looking down benignly on them. It gave Doris a guilty buzz to think of their shared secret. Then she noticed Alb watching Tundra, his expression vitriolic.

'Bernard, you can stop this silly nonsense right now, lad!'

Ignoring him she pecked her mother's cheek, 'shouldn't be too late back, Mum. See you.'

It was after Sunday lunch and Alb decreed that, while their mother washed up, the girls were to get changed. He wanted to build a low wall by the rhubarb. They all went upstairs but he was taken aback when Bernardine reappeared in alien clothes, and wearing a shoulder bag where previously she carried a rucksack.

'What d'you think you're up to, lad?' he snapped, pointing to her dress. He only ever saw her in the one she wore to church. 'Is this your idea of a joke?'

She took no notice of him, checked the contents of her bag.

'You're not going out like that.' He stood over her, hands on hips. She put on her jacket. He snorted at Doris, his arms windmilling.

'You speak to him, woman. Tell him! What does he look like? A big girl's blouse, that's what!'

'Alb, please - ' said Doris faintly.

Bernardine made for the front door. Alb barred her way, his back to it.

'You're not going to disgrace me going out like that. If you want to leave this house you'll dress correctly.'

Bernardine gave him a glance of utter contempt, shrugged her shoulders. Went into the front room, slamming the door.

'He'll come to his senses when he's recovered from his tantrum. He wants to grow up instead of making this stupid carry on.' Alb crossed his arms and stayed where he was to prevent any sudden dash. He picked up the newspaper, started to read it.

After ten minutes he went into the front room expecting a subdued Bernardine, ready to slink off and change. The room was empty, a chair by the open window. He dashed out in time to see her turning the corner out of the Close, skirts fluttering about her legs.

'You know what I put it down to?' Alb shouted at Doris, 'he's gone and inherited your nerves. It made you crackers that time and now he's gone the same way.'

Doris concentrated on her knitting, keeping her thoughts to herself. Next second it was snatched from her hands.

'Answer me when I speak to you, woman!'

He dragged the cardigan sleeve off the needles, pulling the lines of stitches until the piece was unravelled. When it was a tangled mess he threw it on the floor. She watched in silence. Without trembling.

'Who did he say was nuts?' Casey asked her. 'C'mon. We're getting out of here.'

Doris stood up and left the room. When he came ranting after her she went upstairs and locked herself in the bathroom.

CHAPTER TWELVE

'Lavender,' said Tundra, dabbing oil on the hankie and passing it to Doris. 'Deep sniffs before you start to keep you calm. You'll be fine.'

They were sitting in the office of the Test Centre waiting for Doris to go into the exam room for her written driving test. As applicants were seated in alphabetical order they were at the end of the queue.

It was a mere six weeks since they'd collected the car. In that time Doris was amazed to discover she had an aptitude for driving. They'd visited the airfield several times but her first sorties on to a real road were nerve wracking. Tundra soothed her, took her to a quiet district at ten in the morning to start with. Gradually, sitting with her friend, getting the vehicle to do what she wanted, wrought a change in Doris. From living in a state of continual fear she had a measure of control over her life and Rosie was now an important part of it.

Keeping her activities secret from Alb proved easier than expected. She supposed it was because he would never believe her capable of such a thing. For each lesson she and Tundra met at the house where the car was parked and drove to an area where she wouldn't be seen by anyone who knew her.

Doris, who never asserted herself, now insisted she would only accept help if Tundra allowed her to repay her in kind. She'd taken on many of the household chores at Number Seven which gave Tundra more time to paint. A discreet slipping through the hedge avoided other neighbours noticing her coming and going and remarking on it to Alb. Being in the Tyler house was a treat, the two women chatting as they worked at their disparate tasks. Doris would cook them a simple lunch, pick up Tundra's shopping the days she was in college. Finding she could shop successfully made her realise she could budget as well as Alb, better in some cases. Flex was away on tour so she hadn't got to know him but she liked Germayn who, when he was there, treated her as a proper person.

Sometimes her reluctance to leave was so strong she had to force herself home. The girls all knew about her unapproved friendship, but not what was behind it. The times Alb was safely absent they took to popping in to see Tundra themselves, for one reason or another. Harriet and Germayn were working on the performance, Erica and Bernardine came for a chat and because the atmosphere was more congenial at Number Seven.

It was fascinating to listen to Tundra talk about her past. Apart from her travels round the world she had an unusual family history. Her parents were naturists who ran their own colony in The Isle Of Wight. Her mother was also a witch who practised healing and passed on her herbal knowledge to her daughter. After her father's death at eighty, in a sky diving accident, her mother had formed a menage a trois with a pair of twin brothers in their thirties and still lived with them.

So there were times when all the female members of the Wakes family were assembled in Tundra's house. Mr McCloud, who managed the building society sometimes called. He was apparently still suffering the effects of it being robbed at gunpoint, seeing two security men shot, even though he was unharmed. Tundra was giving him massages and diet advice.

The great, glowing stove of her nature drew others to warm themselves at it. She was the presiding spirit of Number Seven as Alb was of Number Nine, where his dominance was stamped on every brick. But things were changing.

By now it was the end of May, the heat bursting everything into flower. It was always Bernardine's favourite time at the garden centre, busy but enjoyable. Sun warmed, the customers were in better temper than during the winter, carrying away their treasure boxes of colour and waving shrubs. Many families made a visit to Land o' Green a day out, bringing the children to look at the fish and reptiles, eat in the cafe. There was a relaxed liveliness to the days.

Or maybe, she thought it was a reflection of the way her own feelings had changed. Because of the increased workload she and Shaun weren't seeing much of each other during the day. But they had got into the custom of going for a drink after work, to talk things over. The frosting of reserve on both their natures was melting.

She learned he'd known his wife from when they were at school. The night she left him to go off with the other man, taking the boys, he came home to find a note. 'I was poleaxed, gutted at the time,' he said. It was apparent to Bernardine he was still recuperating from the damage. She wondered if they could ever repair it.

She was getting to know his children. Since meeting at the narrow boat rally they had been on several outings together. That first time she had been very shy, awkward with them. But Neil, the youngest had climbed quite naturally on to her knee when they sat on the steps of the amphitheatre to watch the clowns and acrobats. When a stilt-walker singled out his brother for teasing the elder boy had got frightened so she held him to her. Their small bodies resting against her made an odd sensation well up, akin to what she felt for Shaun, but gentler. It was an amplification many times of the tenderness she felt for her fragile young plants.

Last Sunday she was taken to meet Shaun's parents. They were like him, quiet, reassuringly normal. She couldn't help her shyness but as soon as she saw the magical garden at the back of their council house she knew they were destined to become friends.

Her greatest difficulty was telling Shaun about herself. How did she explain her father? She tried to give the impression he was merely eccentric. But when she said hesitantly, 'my Dad treats my sisters and me like blokes.

He doesn't like having daughters,' and filled in details, Shaun looked startled. Now she was reluctant for him to meet Alb in case he thought madness ran in the family.

When Tundra's advice was sought she said they would have to come face to face at some point and it might as well be sooner than later. But relations between Bernardine and her father were at an all time low. She was struggling against a lifetime's ingrained subservience, kept telling herself she didn't have to obey his orders. But she and the others would find themselves bullied into working at St. Chad's yet again.

Then the vicar told them of his plans for the bequest money. As there was no room for technical maneouvres at the back of the stage the building was to be extended with rehearsal and dressing rooms, storage for props built on.

'My trusty troop will be at your service,' Alb used his jovial voice. 'Whenever you want us.' The girls exchanged glances.

'Ah. Er, you've worked like Trojans,' Mr Coulson turned to them, 'but I do think you ladies have earned a break. The job entails some heavyweight carpentry. Not that women aren't capable but now as we can afford contractors why not use them. Plus, some of the lads signed up for the drama group have volunteered to build the stage. It's good for these young people to make their contribution.' Seeing Alb's expression he hurried on, 'with you in charge of operations of course, Albert. It needs your expertise to see it through.'

Nonetheless, Alb tried to keep his daughters slogging by marking out the giant rockery. Along the grapevine the vicar heard and asked him to put it on hold in case a larger car park was needed. The girls detected Tundra's influence.

Alb then found odd jobs the neighbours wanted doing. Several times when he told the girls to get into overalls Bernardine went to her room and refused to come down. Although he raged and sneered, she began going out each Sunday.

Her new strategy was to leave straight from church. When she walked past the van Alb tried to stop her in the road with pious utterances.

'Bernard, what do they teach in there?' He jerked a thumb at St. Chad's. 'Honour thy father! You have no right to behave this way.'

'I have every right.' She hurried to Shaun's car waiting opposite, got in. As they drove away she saw her father in the wing mirror, a barbed wire figure.

'Of course you've done it.' Tundra gazed with satisfaction at the paper stating that Mrs Doris Wakes had passed the written section of the driving test. 'I was sure you would.'

'I wasn't. I could never remember answers to anything at school.'

'No doubt they asked you the wrong questions. Now, until we've got a date for your on-road test we'll put in every minute of practice we can.'

'I still feel I'm using your time, taking you from painting.'

'Nobody's allowed to do that. It gives me a break to get out with you. Besides, look at the way you're preventing my place descending into a pigsty.'

Bernardine finally brought Shaun home one weekday after work. Her sisters, forewarned, greeted him with warmth, intrigued at Bernie having a bloke but Doris looked worried, glancing out of the window. Alb, at the end of the garden among the fruit bushes, had not been warned of the visit. Now or never, Bernardine thought, and led Shaun out to meet him, the others following at a distance. Alb glanced up, startled as the five of them approached, one a stranger he didn't like the look of.

'Dad,' said Bernardine, 'this is my friend, Shaun. Shaun, my father.'

The reason for what he regarded as Bernard's insolence

suddenly clicked into place. Alb wore the distaste of one trying to unblock a drain as he scowled at their entwined hands. He gave Shaun a jerk of his head, more a sign of dismissal than greeting.

'Nice garden,' the visitor tried as an opening gambit, 'I'd heard you were keen.'

Alb eyed him with dislike. He may as well have said, 'I'd heard you were a bastard.'

'Your blackcurrant bushes are very vigorous,' Shaun remarked.

'I planted those,' Bernardine couldn't help adding, with a touch of pride. 'We get a good crop. Oh - ' She noticed her father had been digging round one of the bushes, exposing the roots. No point in asking why. She knew.

'I like their smell, don't you?' Shaun continued to play the guest, pulled off a leaf, sniffed it.

It was as though he had tweaked Alb's nose. 'No, I'm sick of the horrible things. I'm taking the lot up. The lot!' he snarled.

He grabbed the spade he had been using and attacked the bush, slashing and hacking at it. He paused to give it a tug but it remained rooted.

'A pity to destroy a healthy plant.' Shaun couldn't hide his annoyance.

'It doesn't want to come out.' Bernardine touched the mutilated bush.

'We'll see about that!' bawled Alb and bounded into the shed.

Next minute he reappeared with his Agri Claw, a garden tool with a short handle and four sharp offset prongs for loosening stubborn roots and tussocks. He stabbed the crumbly ground under the bush. With all his strength he worked it back and forth, worrying the roots, growling with the effort, occasionally tearing at the branches with his hands. Bernardine and Shaun stood close together, watching in amazed silence, Doris and the girls retreated to the back door.

In one furious, superhuman pounce Alb grabbed the whole bush and it came away. Swinging it round his head he shouted, 'to Hell with this rubbish!' and tossed it upwards. The blackcurrant meteorite zoomed a showering arc of soil through the air and crashed through the greenhouse roof.

There was a nano-second of dismay before Alb, teeth bared, glared at the Claw, shook it, then glared at the onlookers. He held the implement in front of him. Advanced on them. 'See? See this?' They all jumped in alarm.

He was about to vent his fury by a rant at poorly designed tools, make them see its inferiority up close, whilst implying it was on a par with their own. But Shaun was not to know this. Alb's gangling figure, an X of fury in black overalls, brandishing the tool, caused him an horrific memory flash. He lived again the blinding terror his five-year-old self felt at the pantomime when Captain Hook came towards Peter Pan, about to do him in.

Pushing Bernardine to safety he leapt at Alb, tried to wrest the Claw off him, hanging on to stop him using it on them. The two men scuffled to and fro, struggling for possession, kicking up clouds of dust. The veins on Alb's forehead stood out as he resisted but Shaun was the stronger. By kneeing Alb in the groin he won the Claw, but in doing so fell backwards, lost it as it shot through the air in the other direction and demolished the kitchen window in a shatter of glass.

Alb was speechless for several seconds, his features appearing to implode as, eyes bulging, teeth clenched, he held his crutch and did a choking dance across the lawn. At last he found his voice.

'My God!' he gave a strangled scream, 'my God! Did you see that, Dor? Have you seen what your lad's turned into? Someone who dresses like a nancy boy then brings his hooligan mates home to attack his parents!'

Shaun jumped to his feet, also blazing with anger.

Bernardine hugged sobs of shame. He put protective arms round her, glared back at Alb. 'Speak to her like that again and I'll bloody punch out your tripes! You're insane, Mr Wakes. You need locking up!' He turned to Barnardine, 'come on, sweetheart. We're getting out of this.'

He shepherded her into the house, followed by the others who glanced back, chastened, at Alb. He didn't come after them but got a hammer and attacked the kitchen window, knocking out the jags of glass. They heard his demented banging as they huddled in the hall, the front door open. Shaun stood, arms folded, as Bernardine ran upstairs and stuffed things into her rucksack.

'I'm taking her to my flat, Mrs Wakes. You can't expect her to tolerate this.'

'No, of course not.' Doris shook her head. Casey's whisper echoed in her skull, 'this is your fault. You could have stopped the rot years ago. It should've been you who kicked him in the balls.'

Bernardine, loaded with bags, dashed downstairs into Shaun's embrace. She was breathless as she turned to hug her mother and sisters.

'I'll be in touch, Mum. I'll see you when he's not around, pick up the rest of my stuff.'

They crammed to the front gate, waved as she and Shaun got in the car. Then she was gone.

'Now there's one less to spread the load,' Erica said to Harriet as they sat gloomily in the back bedroom. 'Of course I don't blame Bernie but it could get grim.'

Since their association with the Tylers it had become easier for the sisters to talk freely. In all the years at Number Nine they and Doris had been separated from each other in the struggle to survive. Each of them needing every scrap of energy, their sense of self preservation, to live with the scourging anger directed at them.

As well as dropping into her house for coffee, Erica

chatted with Tundra in the art department at college whenever she got the chance. Tundra had been told about Gareth and her wish to emulate him and had been helpful with addresses where Erica might apply for help.

'The problem is though, I'll be financially dependent on Dad. He'll try to stop me.'

'There are ways. You could leave home, lodge with other students, get a loan and a part time job.'

'I'd love to but he wouldn't - '

'Allow it? After your birthday it's up to you. Maybe your mother will get a job and help.'

'Mum?' Erica laughed. 'She's the problem. I can't leave her to his mercy.' The idea of her mouse of a parent having a job was preposterous. Her mother was the one they all had to look out for. It was the only reason she herself put up with her father.

Now, absently fondling a Barbie, Harriet said, 'he's not going to stop me going to my class.' They both grimaced. It was a joke. Harriet had worked out an ingenious way to spend time working with Germayn. When she told Alb she'd be doing extra studying he turned his searchlight of suspicion on her.

'Learn tailoring? There's no need when you've got a job.'

'But this is day release from Spraffy's. By improving my skills I get on a higher rate of pay.'

'It means a drop in your money now then?'

'If I work on my days off I can make it up.'

'On Saturdays? No. There are things you're needed for at St. Chad's.'

'I don't think so, Dad. I've spoken to Mr Coulson about it and he told me the Jones twins and Jack Fletcher will be helping you. He agreed I should try to further my career.'

Alb did an apoplectic splutter, 'you went to the vicar behind my back, lad!'

'He was coming out of Mrs Tyler's so I had a word,' she

spoke quietly, 'ask him. See what he says.'

Where she was really spending time was at the television studios in town, attending rehearsals with Germayn. Her boss was almost as enthusiastic over showbiz as herself and had been supportive, making flexi hours for her. On the nights Alb was out, or even sometimes when he wasn't she slipped next door so they could work on the act. It was fortunate that he never went in their rooms as Doris was able to use the alibi that she was in bed with another headache.

Since that first visit to Saucy Girls the rapport between herself and Germayn had grown. Because Alb was at Tool Magic all day that Easter Saturday, she skipped the church hall and spent the day next door. Tundra's laughter had rumbled through the house as she made merry with Flex, his group and other friends in her parlour but Harriet and Germayn sat at the dining table as he talked her through the act he was going to use in the Dreamstars show.

He brought out a stack of scrapbooks of shows he'd been in, going back to infant school. Together they picked over them for inspiration.

'I think your performance is good, Germayn, but, don't take this wrong, it's not brilliant. You need to make it more original.'

'Yes, I know. Y'see there are five contestants in each show and I said to Mumzo, I suspect they're only using me to make up numbers. The other four people are two singers, a hand puppet and a stand-up. Throw in the drag act for variety, eh?'

'That's ridiculous when you were chosen from thousands of others. You can be better than them. But not by playing this scrubber housewife character. I think Lily Savage is great, a really strong image. You won't get anywhere trying to be a pale copy of her.'

He nodded, chin in hands. He seemed despondent as she flicked another page. 'Don't know how to improve my repertoire in such a short time.'

'We'll come up with something if we try.' She turned another page, 'that one's gorgeous,' she pointed to a photo of him wearing a gown with a fishtail train.

'That was when I used to do my Marilyn. Now she's a bit passé.'

'It's like one I made Tartine.'

'Who?'

'Oh, er, one of my girls. I mean, she's a doll,' Germayn looked quizzical. Harriet made up her mind. 'Come on, I'll show you.'

Erica and Doris had taken the List on its pilgrimage to the supermarket so the house was empty as he followed her up to the bedroom.

'This is my half,' she explained. 'And this is my collection.'

'Wow! Phew.' He stared in amazement.

She passed them down for him to examine.

'They're so beautiful. Oh, look at her. I love that one.' Harriet was gratified at such sincere admiration of her handiwork as he turned them round, exclaimed over the clothes.

'I can scale any of the designs up to fit you. Which one d'you think?'

'I want them all.' Germayn sighed with pleasure as he held them up one after another. Harriet grinned. Someone other than Ann understood what it was about.

'I haven't shown you Tartine. There, above the door. I'll pass the chair. But he could reach. He gazed, then slowly lifted the doll from her shrine, made a reverent, soundless O.

'Harriet, she's incredible. Those legs, the face, that red silk with the purple bodice. What did you say her name is?'

'Tartine Zircon. I made it up. She's got a much larger wardrobe than the rest.' She wondered if she could risk telling him. 'My mate, Ann, and I make up soap operas about the girls, just for fun. Tartine's had a hard life but she's a survivor, a real tryer. If she was starving she'd rather

158

buy a lipstick than a loaf, clings to her glamour even when she's down on her luck.'

Germayn looked from the doll to Harriet and back. Their eyes widened as the thought struck them at the same instant. 'Of course!'

'There's only a few weeks. D'you want to go for it? Will they let you change the act?'

'I'm not sure but let's do it. I mean, it was about me as a performer. It's not like I've changed the type of act.'

'You'll still sing that song, but as Tartine, glamour girl down on her uppers.'

'Will they let me change my script, my look? It isn't possible in the time, Harriet.'

Harriet went to her resources drawer, took hold of the material she had found irresistible the day Ann called. She billowed it over Germayn who caught it, felt it against his face.

'You'll need a darker panstick, of course. Have you a wig like that?'

'What about the script? It took me ages thinking what to say.'

'Let's get cracking on your gown and decide the scenario as we work.' She picked up a tape-measure, used it along one of his arms, made technical enquiries about bosom size, noted things down. 'Come along. I'll need your waist and hips to be accurate.'

Germayn unbuttoned his jeans. 'D'you mind? I mean your old man's a bit of a religious nut, isn't he?'

'Don't be silly. I've seen many an actor in their undies.'

He lifted his tee shirt, dropped the jeans to his knees as she ran the tape round him. She regarded him appreciatively but only in an aesthetic sense. She was akin to an artist who, after years of being obliged to draw on the back of postcards, is suddenly presented with a door-sized canvas.

Feverishly they co-operated on the costume, sketched what was wanted in record time. Then Harriet was cutting,

159

pinning, Germayn ironing the pieces, tacking them, as though the pair of them were contestants on some have-a-go game show. Their fingers flew, with quick checks for adjustments in the mirror, while they talked and argued on how to project Tartine. Germayn stood her on the windowsill and they kept glancing up at her with affection.

'She's my top favourite,' said Harriet. 'Sometimes she's more real to me than people I know. It's like I go with her into her world. A real living doll.'

'Hey!' In unison they paused, stared at each other again.

'That's it. You don't go on as a woman but as a living doll!'

'But a doll for grown ups. One who goes through all the hassle, the angst.'

They were chattering excitedly at each other.

'You scribble this down whilst I sew. Now, let's see, she deals with other dolls who bitch or are her friends.'

'And other toys. How about the lecherous cloth rabbit who runs the corner shop, her yobbish robot landlord -'

'Wait, we'll give her a catchphrase. Er...hmm...how about, 'come here, Toy Boy. I've got a new battery in.'

'Or maybe, 'time for beddy, Teddy Bear.'

'Brilliant. Yes, that one.'

They heard someone come in downstairs.

'God, it's not your father?'

Harriet checked, 'no.' She came down with Germayn after her as Doris and Erica turned, surprised.

'Erica, Mum, will you keep a secret?'

In an intensive month Harriet and Germayn brought Tartine to life. At the television studios there was some grumbling over the change to Germayn's act. When he and Harriet were summoned to a script meeting to discuss it, they were fearful it would be scrapped. But the producer decided the revised act was better than the audition piece that got Germayn selected. He could see the Tartine character made for a better programme.

Harriet went with Germayn to as many rehearsals as she could, coaching, encouraging. The two of them knew they were fortunate living on the doorstep of the television company. Contestants travelled from all over the country. Opposite the towering company headquarters the rehearsal studios were in a converted schoolhouse. It had served the vanished residential district the area had once been. Now every erstwhile classroom was alive with dancers, singers, people constructing scenery, wails and shouts of actors practising lines, groups round tables arguing over scripts. As they passed open doors Germayn and Harriet swapped a look of excitement.

In what had obviously been the pupils' assembly hall the contestants met with Jules, their director. All of them except the comedian had brought helpers but it was tacitly understood that these would stay in the background, not try to intervene in any way, fetch and carry and do as Jules told them.

'Obviously each of you sees your own performance as the most important part of the show,' he said to Germayn and the others. 'You must take on board I have to balance all the acts into a cohesive entertainment. And the public gets upset if we even appear to favour one person more than another. So it may be necessary to change a detail here and there.'

'Don't like the sound of that,' whispered Germayn.

'Stop worrying, we'll work round it,' Harriet answered.

There was also a musical director and two wardrobe assistants working with the group. Germayn wore an ex-Saucy Girls outfit to rehearse but Harriet had to bring in the Tartine dress she'd made him for the experts to approve. They didn't want Germayn's shoulders to be bare so they altered it on the premises. When she got home Harriet added a replica of the sleeves they'd made to the Tartine doll.

Jules decided the running order of acts was singer,

comedian, tap dancer, singer, Germayn, and worked them hard all morning. Harriet could see some of them getting very uptight, trying to conceal it. Working at home with Germayn she was able to keep his confidence level topped up. Here nobody was given special treatment and, after Jules had made him re-do one of his lines eight times, he was on the verge of tears.

She came expecting fierce rivalry amongst the contestants but found a cameraderie between everyone that reminded her of the the time she was in hospital to have her tonsils out. There was the same supportiveness from fellow patients, all of them there to get through an ordeal.

At midday they went to the ground floor of the old school, transformed into a club and restaurant for company employees and visiting artists. Sitting with their salads, Germayn and Harriet scanned the room, celebrity spotting. Two soap opera characters who had been coming into the Wakes' living room as old friends for years, sat at the bar with their pints. Three members of Manchester's top boy band were tucking into fish and chips as the fourth returned from the loo. A newscaster was talking deferentially to a blonde woman in a suit, probably his boss, Harriet decided. It wasn't her lunch she wanted to eat. It was all of this.

She revelled in the electrifying atmosphere pervading the whole complex, a sense of something marvellous about to happen. Here among the actors, technicians, make-up artists, was her home. Her best moment came when a singer asked Germayn if she was his dresser.

'Yes. And my friend, coach and co-writer.'

Every spare moment they could be in Number Seven without Alb knowing they rehearsed. Harriet found Germayn responded best if he was coaxed to go over the moves, the words again and again. By the time the date of the show arrived they'd created something as perfect as they could make it.

For the performance Germayn got tickets for his mother, the vicar, Ann, the boss of Spraffy's and Harriet to be in the studio audience. She would, of course, be backstage but her ticket was to salve Mr Coulson's conscience. At Tundra's urging, he told Alb he was including Harriet in his party as the show was relevant to her work, which was not strictly lying.

'No offence, vicar,' Alb said stiffly, 'but I won't let my offspring witness lewd behaviour. The Good Book definitely states wearing clothes of the other sex is a sin.'

'I'm surprised to hear you say that, Albert. Cross dressing is an ancient tradition, you know. In Greek theatre male actors played women. Then of course we have Shakespeare.'

'I live by scripture, not people who write plays.'

'In any case, you can't forbid Harriet to go wherever she chooses. She is past her majority.'

Alb didn't trust himself to speak, nodding as if resigned when, in fact, he was trying to stop himself choking.

It was the cue call. Time to go on. After hours of careful arranging, brushing, primping, Germayn was turned into Tartine Zircon, life-size, living. But she showed very human nerves. A make-up assistant dashed forward to sponge the sweat off her forehead. Harriet squeezed Tartine's hand and began the warm-up they had practised between them.

'You're a gorgeous girl. Repeat.'

'I'm gorgeous.'

'You've more talent than anyone here.'

'I've got oodles of talent.'

'You're gonna go out there and give it to 'em.'

'I'll knock 'em dead.' The voice became more resolute as Harriet led the string of affirmations. She accompanied the vivid, lofty figure to the performance area where they waited as the previous performer finished.

Assistants handed Tartine onto the set. In the spotlight, her music playing, she was the teendoll, funny, making sassy comments on life. Watching her, Harriet lived every tiny gesture, every intonation through the nerve wracking four minutes. Tartine captivated them, threw them into fits of laughter, held them spellbound as she finished with her plaintive keeping-your-chin-up song.

In the heats it was the studio audience that chose the top act. It was only for the final that a viewers poll was used too.

Her mother and sisters had been going to watch the show on television but Alb grimly turned to another channel. Although they couldn't see it live they knew it would be on Tundra's video for later. However, Erica borrowed Clare's mobile phone so she and Doris knew the result as soon as it came through.

The report of Germayn's success, with a photo of him in character, appeared in a couple of national tabloids next day. Lily Wakes had seen the show and rang Alb to say the paper said that Tartine Zircon, who had tickled her, lived in Riffton and did he know her?

No, Alb told her, he didn't.

CHAPTER THIRTEEN

Since Bernardine's departure the house had developed an echo. Her vacant chair at the table, her garden boots gone from their place in the scullery. There were closed looks on the faces of the remaining women when they were with Alb. Nobody mentioned her and Shaun in his presence but their wall of silent disapproval was as loud as if they stood yelling at him. Bernardine had actually rung several times when he was out, to reassure Doris.

'I had to go, Mum, even though I hate leaving you with him.'

'He's suffering bad toothache so he's been quieter than usual.'

'I'm living with Shaun from now on. We've decided we've a future together, Mum. You'll come and visit when we're settled? You and Erica and Harriet?'

'Of course we will, love. God bless.'

She was relieved at her daughter's escape yet felt the loss of her. What would there ever have been for her here? Doris thought. It was impossible to imagine her having the normal courtship she obviously craved.   ' A wedding in St. Chad's? That's a laugh,' said Casey from behind her. 'Can you see the bride's father, "who gives this lad? I'm losing a son and gaining a son." '

Doris sighed. Of all of them he'd made Bernardine, the quietest, most acquiescent, suffer the most.

Now Bernardine had left, she knew the others would soon follow. They had found their courage. And what then? She looked into the future, finding the thought of herself and Alb growing old together, just the two of them in Number Nine, totally unbearable.

When she expressed worries about affording the upkeep of Rosie once the year was up, Tundra said, 'you can earn your own money.'

'Me? What can I do? I'm too old and I've no

qualifications.'

'For starters you're a good cleaner and housekeeper. The college advertises for kitchen staff all the time. Then, if you wanted to try other things there are free training courses you can go on. I'll get you details.' She's a magician, Doris thought, always conjuring good ideas out of those scarves.

'A cancellation?' Doris fisted hands to her face later the same day. They had prudently put Tundra's phone number on the driving test application form and now she was relaying the message.

'You're booked for nine-thirty tomorrow. The hordes of mums and school kids are out of the way then. Don't look like that. You're fine.'

'Alb's got an appointment with the dentist mid morning. He's going straight from work. What if he decides to come home?'

'You're going to have to tell Alb at some point, Doris. Choose the moment carefully, but do it.'

As they drove to the Test Centre she was apprehensive, as when she had had to go to the doctor for check-ups on her nerves, all that time ago. The nerves had been controlled. But they seemed to form an underground movement, always there threatening to break out and terrorize her again, specially when Alb shouted. She turned to Tundra who gave her a melon slice smile. Doris returned it. Since Tundra appeared, her nerves had retreated into the distance; troublesome relatives who had emigrated, still alive but out of the vicinity. She braced herself, trying to stay calm, to remember all her friend had taught her.

Alb's jaw and one ear throbbed as he used a labelling gun in the timber section. He had insisted on coming in to work because of his unshakeable conviction the place would collapse without his presence for at least part of the day.

News of a sensational scandal was buzzing through Tool Magic. The boss's wife of twenty years had left him for another woman. He hadn't an inkling until it happened because his wife's lover was his sister. He'd thought they just liked to go on hiking and shopping trips together until he got the divorce papers. They'd stripped the house of every valuable while he was out, even taking his fish tank and the parrot. Now he was receiving counselling and on Prozac.

This state of affairs increased Alb's gloom. He was trying to ignore a deep unease at the recent changes in his own life. He'd thought everything decent, respectable, then, boom, it shattered. He knew himself to be a righteous man who followed the teachings of the Good Book as he'd been taught. He'd disciplined his family in order to keep Sodom and Gomorrah out of the home and it came to live next door. Forcefully he slapped a sticker on a length of dowel.

Last night, at a meeting the vicar called to discuss the alterations, Alb's new helpers were introduced to him. He could tell at once they weren't prepared to obey orders in the same way as his own lads. They were decidedly over-familiar, one even giving him a playful punch on the arm. It would be difficult keeping control. What's more he didn't like to think about his own lads, how far they'd gone off the rails. Rick and Harry were never there, not openly disobeying orders but dodging them. The other one was a complete write-off. Having a father who'd always tried to be an example to him obviously hadn't been enough. Good riddance to a bad apple. From now on he only had two sons.

He suspected they were all hatching plots against him at Number Nine but Doris worried him the most. She still did as she was told yet there was something different in the way she did it. Deferential, that was it. She wasn't as deferential these days. And she should be. She had a good husband who'd spent a lifetime protecting and training her. He gave an involuntary shiver. Last night, unable to sleep

167

for toothache, he had been dozing fitfully when she disturbed him by talking in her sleep.

'Fourth,' she'd mumbled. 'Again. Again! Back round that corner...mmm.'

The fourth of what? The fourth time for what? Which corner?

Then, as he watched her sleeping face she had cried out the name of a woman.

'Rosie. My Rosie.' There was a sentimental note to it.

A wave of cold sank over him. He had a mind to shake her conscious but something stopped him. He watched her for quite a long time.

'Whoooo- !' Tundra swung Doris off her feet, thudded a kiss on her. 'I'm so pleased for you. All done in record time, too. Not many achieve that.'

'I thought I'd failed. The examiner told me off for not using mirrors enough. He was really severe. Then he said, "I'm pleased to tell you that you've passed, Mrs Wakes," and shook my hand.' Doris felt oddly shy at her unexpected triumph. She was shaking with relief and delight.

'These fellows have to get off on their little moments of power. The important thing is that you've got your licence.'

They walked over to where Rosie, gleamed in the morning sun. Tundra bent to replace the L plates with green ones. 'There you go. She's all yours now.' She got into the passenger seat and opened the driver's door for Doris to get behind the wheel. 'I'd suggest going for a run but I haven't time today. To Piccadilly Station please, Driver.'

'Why there?'

'To catch my train of course, I've an appointment at a gallery in Oldham who're showing my work.' Doris had been too preoccupied before to notice the portfolio by Tundra's feet. 'I'm only taking along photos and sketches with me today. I'm on the ten thirty.'

'But that means I -'

'Drive back on your own. Yes. You don't need me here any more. You did it, Doris. You can fly, little bird.' She flapped meaty hands.

Doris tried to share the joke but was gulping down panic. Driving with another, competent person beside you was one thing. There was always that feeling it was a shared responsibility, they would bale you out if you made a mistake. But now, here was Doris Wakes, going to be let loose on her own. On an innocent public.

She had been so busy learning to drive, memorizing the Highway Code, concealing her movements from Alb, she hadn't cast her mind that far ahead. When she wasn't with Tundra, whose presence infused her with confidence, the whole thing had seemed an impossible dream, a fantasy. The spectres of the nuns, of Alb, of Lily telling her how stupid she was had to be constantly pushed out of her mind when she was alone.

'It isn't so impossible after all. I'm with you,' said Casey. 'I'll see you're okay.' After dropping Tundra off, Doris did a couple of circuits of the city centre without hitting anything, then headed back to Riffton. By the time she reached it, the exhilaration of driving Rosie had got to her. Lovely feeling. Somehow the car herself had taken over the role of second companion after Casey. 'That's it. Good girl, Rosie.' Doris was in a private space that was hers alone. Nobody to ridicule her. No Alb. Not wanting to stop, she went weaving up and down the side roads, exulting in this heady partnership.

Alb, coming out of the dentist's, had a frozen lip from the injection. Getting teeth filled always left him whoozy from the effort of concealing his fright from the attractive dental nurse. He would sit in the van a minute, blow that surgery smell out of his nostrils. As he opened his door a red car went past with Doris driving it. He shook his head to clear it, stop himself imagining things. No, of course it wasn't

her, he frowned after it. But when it reached the bottom of
the road a doubt niggled his mind. He jumped in the van
and followed, just to confirm to himself that he was right.
You often saw someone who was the image of another
person and it surprised you for a moment, he told himself.
Of course it wasn't her. Ridiculous idea.

Doris had glimpsed Alb in the mirror and was seized by
her old fear. There would be such a scene. He mustn't know
yet. She put on a spurt and turned up the road to the rugby
fields. She was delayed by having to get out and open the
gate of Mr McCloud's house but she managed to park Rosie
at breakneck speed then dash towards Turvey Close. As
she ran she tore up sprays of wild flowers, stopped, got her
breath, and was sniffing them as the van passed her,
strolling with her bouquet towards Number Nine. It was
fortunate he couldn't hear her heart pounding, the lung
fulls of air she drew in. As if just spotting him she went to
perform the carport ritual.

'Hello, Alb. How did you get on? Fillings?'

'Yes. Get me an aspirin.' As they went in he closely
scanned her small, spare person, her lank hair. She was as
weak as ever. Ineffectual. She was still his Dor the way he
permitted her to be. The recent upsets were making him
imagine things. That was it, she was still pining because of
that lad leaving but she'd get over it, as she'd done with
other matters. He was boss round here.

Later that evening his toothache had subsided and he
pottered in the garden. He found it progressively more
uncomfortable to be in the house, the underlying
atmosphere irritating. He couldn't go to the hall either, as
there was a Women's Institute meeting tonight, the last
permitted use before they closed it for the renovations.

Harriet was out but Erica and her mother were watching
a comedy programme that had been yellow markered,
about veterinary surgeons in Yorkshire. He liked it too but

didn't want to sit with them. The sky was turning deep plum, a moon rising, but the air was hot as he took a manual trimmer and inspected the hedge on the Tylers' side for rogue leaves. There were none. It could have been clipped by the National Trust. It was very high but he wished he didn't even have to see the roof of that disgusting woman's house, be reminded of her existence. All the things that had gone wrong had happened since she took over. She and her brood were scum. They didn't belong in the Close.

As he worked his way along the hedge a slight flash of something on the other side caught his attention. He searched for an opening in the tightly packed foliage through which to see, pulled some twigs apart. Gaped. No! He caught glimpses of Tundra, quite naked, arranging candles on a patio table. The rest of her garden was also enclosed by the hedge, making it totally private. An impulse made him strain to see fully. He could not. Before he admitted to himself what he was doing he rushed into the house and bounded upstairs.

The landing window was the only one from which it was possible to see into next door's garden. The glass itself was opaqued by a raised bubble pattern so he grabbed a box on legs that hid loo rolls in the bathroom, and stood on it to look through the opening window at the top.

A large cherry tree was in his line of vision, but in her passing and re-passing vignettes of Tundra were framed by the branches. He goggled at her. Naked she was even more massive. In the flickering light she looked the statue of a primitive goddess, devouring deity to a cannibal tribe. A roll of fat like an ornamental swag festooned her stomach, her limbs were pocked with dimples. The most surprising features were her breasts, quite high and solid; gun emplacements. The nipples: warheads pointing outwards, unlike the two dying animals hanging from the chest wall he so often saw in large women. She herself had the look of a huge waxen candle, a monolithic Venus with silver head. How dare she go round like that. She was a sink of moral pollution, he raged to himself, The Whore of Babylon had taken over Turvey Close. He went hot as, to his horror, there was a sudden hardening in his trousers.

'Coming to join me, darling?' He broke into a sweat as she spoke, thinking she could see him.

Then his mouth fell open. A second naked figure joined her. The man she was speaking to came through the French windows with a drinks tray, put it on the table and opened a bottle of wine. He poured two drinks and they clinked glasses as he embraced her. Alb's heart bumped with fright, with utter dismay. It was the manager of his building society!

After his mother, Alb's money was his greatest concern. When he was made redundant from the kitchen firm many years ago, he'd salted the severance pay into the coffers of the Norfax, adding to it each month; safe in the knowledge it was secured by vaults, by a shield of respectability administered by people in business clothes and clean underwear. Now it was threatened horribly by loose behaviour. The sight of the Norfax manager's penis, lying quietly minding its own business on its sporran of hair, deeply offended him. Filth and corruption everywhere.

'Excuse me, Dad,' said Erica.

He nearly fell off the box. Quickly he banged the window shut.

'Well? What is it?' He struggled to regain his composure.

'I want to get past. To the bathroom.'

'Here. Put this back.' Thrusting the box at her he stamped down to the front room.

Doris, still elated by the day's events, glanced up, saw his face and concentrated on the screen.

When they went to bed he had a nightmare that shook him to the core. He was walking down Riffton high street, naked except for a blackcurrant leaf. It suddenly changed into his Norfax pass book as Tundra came out of a shop and took it off him. He was surrounded by people sniggering, including the vicar and Mrs Copeland, as he began to pee down a grid.

The week previous to the grand final, Harriet and Germayn had taken a few days off from their respective employers to hone the act. In the weeks since winning his heat Germayn had been seized by bouts of skittishness which she was learning to handle. On Thursday he was in a state of near collapse. After the initial win he was approached by an agency that wanted to sign him straight away. Harriet advised him to turn it down. The Dreamstars' first prize was a contract with a much bigger one, with several celebrities on the books. As a long shot she contacted them to see if they would sign him up anyway, but they said they'd only be interested if he was supreme winner. Otherwise it wasn't worth their while. The implications played on his mind.

'The stress does my head in. The thought of all those people watching. And all my friends, everyone at Saucy's rooting for me.' He was lying on the chaise longue as Tundra did reflexology maneouvres on his feet. Following her instructions Harriet had lit a burner of oil to calm him.

Over the previous weeks they watched other contestants winning their heats on TV. Harriet minutely analysed their techniques, comparing and modifying Tartine's act accordingly. Germayn voiced his fears to Tundra. 'It'll be that kid doing the conjuring, I know it. He does the cute bit. Audiences go for cute.' The two singers gave him cause for concern too. 'They're much better than me, Mumzo. Much. And that Geordie impressionist's so accurate, so funny. Why am I bothering? I'll be mortified when everyone sees my spectacular public failure.'

'Stop that.' Harriet was firm, 'this is the same as what you've done before, only on a bigger scale. You're terrific, a real trooper, you know you are.'

Tundra backed her, 'I'll hear no more of that talk either. You were raised to think positive, darling.'

'I can't think at all, I'm so over wound.' He sat up, elegant fingers pressed to his temples.

'We've rehearsed pretty hard,' Harriet said to her. 'What he needs is to go out and completely forget the show for a few hours. Any ideas?'

'What about Ed?' suggested his mother, 'I hear he's opened a gym.'

'Yes', Germayn brightened. 'We were very close at one time,' he explained to Harriet. 'Then someone else got in the way. But I spoke to him recently in a pub and he's still friendly.'

'That's settled. Give him a call and see if you can do a work out with him.' Harriet was concentrating on styling the two wigs, one a spare in case of mishaps, that they were using for the show.

When he returned that evening he was relaxed and his optimism had returned. An afternoon with Ed had obviously worked wonders. Still, thought Harriet, it would be best to make contingency plans.

Harriet had thought to go home for the evening meal each day to give the appearance of having been to Spraffy's, returning to the Tylers afterwards. But Alb's temper had become very unstable since the Agri-Claw incident and she was afraid of him discovering she was supporting Germayn. If he did he would ruin their chances. Slipping through the hedge after her parents and Erica had gone to bed each night she preferred facing his anger at breakfast.

'And what time did you crawl in last night, lad? What's the idea of treating your home like a doss house?'

Harriet had murmured about Spraffy's having an urgent project on hand, to costume a parade being sponsored by the major retailers in town. Everyone was mucking in to give the organisation a boost. The boss had taken them all for a bite afterwards.

But it was only a token snarl on his part. He didn't rant in his usual fashion. Instead there was a prickly sullenness about him which the others accepted with relief. It was a household where they'd long ago learned it was easier to say nothing than constantly monitor yourself in case you came out with the wrong thing.

CHAPTER FOURTEEN

At last the day had arrived. The studio from which their show was to be transmitted was taken up with technical adjustments for sound and lighting so the artists did their run-through in one of the smarter rehearsal rooms in the company building.

Their director drove them hard all morning as Harriet and the other supporters watched from the sidelines. Satisfied everyone was up to scratch he eased off and began joking with them. Harriet noticed the interaction between contestants was not so matey as it had been at the heat show. There was too much riding on this one, the golden ladder beckoning for whoever charmed the studio audience, then the armchair jury of millions watching at home. Each performer carried their talent like a precious egg. The tension around the dressing rooms was so taut it seemed something must break. This time there was the fierceness of unspoken rivalry as they all applauded and praised each other.

Germayn wore a different dress and second-best wig for the final rehearsal. The true impact of Tartine Zircon still hung mysteriously on a plastic-shrouded hanger in Wardrobe. The show was going out at eight o' clock that evening and the full dress and tech rehearsal was to be held at four.

Much later, when the audience were settled in and Tundra had gone to join the vicar and their other friends, stage fright struck Germayn. He was scheduled to go on last and as they sat in the dressing room watching the others on the monitor he got progressively panicky.

'Oh God, Harriet, I can't do it. I can't. I'm petrified.' He was trembling.

She took one of his hands, with its metallic red nails,

massaging it as Tundra had shown her. 'You're all right. You're doing fine. Listen to me, Tartine. You are superb. You are a wonderful living doll who has been through horrendous problems and come out still singing.'

The current act ended in resounding applause as the presenter had a few words with the performer.

'Look at that. They absolutely love him.'

'Come on. You know they're told to clap as loud as possible.'

The next performer came on, a singer with the same swooping variety of voice as Celine Dion. The song had overtones of Celtic sentimentality. Shots of the audience showed them listening, moist-eyed.

'Oh, she's done it. She's got it.' Germayn held his head in his hands.

'No, not original enough. But you are.'

'I can't go out there. I can't force myself. I'm trying to and I can't.' His whole body shook. She pulled him to his feet.

'Walk up and down with me. That's it.'

He did as he was told. She held his convulsively twitching arm.

'I'm petrified.' His stare was wild, 'I never funked a show in my life, honestly.'

'I believe you. And you won't funk this one.'

'I'll die if I go out there.'

His breathing was shallow now, harsh. She got him to blow into a paper bag, wafted essential oil under his nose. She wished Tundra was here instead of in the audience but the rule was only one personal assistant per artist allowed backstage. As the song finished fear began to grip her too. He was on in less than two minutes. She had made sure his costume and make-up were immaculate. He looked stunning. His eyes were glassy with terror. He wasn't Tartine.

Despairingly he slumped against her. Time for the trump card, she decided. She crouched under the make-up table,

177

opened a bag, took out a box. From a tissue cloud the doll emerged. Harriet held her in front of him.

'Look at her. Go on, look.' She shook his shoulder to emphasize her words. 'This is who you are. You're nobody else but Tartine Zircon. You're strong. You're beautiful. You're the funniest woman in this building. Those people need you, Tartine. You've got something very special for them. Your humour. Your heart. Go out and give them the gift of laughter. They want you.'

He took the doll, held her, looked intently into her face. Harriet had been at great pains to match their two costumes, faces, hair in every detail.

'Don't deny your audience, Tartine. Let them have the pleasure of your wonderful performance.'

On the monitor the previous act was taking a bow. The presenter spoke a few complimentary words. Any second he would announce Germayn. An ear-phoned assistant came for him.

He stood up. Before Harriet's anxious gaze he began to dissolve and Tartine Zircon stood there in a blaze of charisma. Harriet had a lump in her throat as she saw the figure around which she'd woven so many imaginings had stepped from her niche. Was life-sized, real. She accompanied her fabulous creature, now walking with composure, along the passage to the stage. The floor manager would allow her no further so she took the doll, held it up. Tartine glanced at her alter ego for a moment then walked confidently into the spotlight.

In the interval before the winner was announced the camera held a shot of the five contestants, guillotine smiles at the ready to congratulate whoever had killed them. The camera zoomed in on Tartine Zircon holding a perfect replica of herself. It cut to the others but came back to her twice.

The presenter stood out front. He looked solemn. 'Studio audience cast your votes - NOW!'

Tartine was an overwhelming triumph, her victory a

landslide.

'It's not for real,' Germayn kept repeating to his mother and Harriet.

There was a somewhat tense party in the studio while the telephone poll was processed. It would be closed and the winner announced in an hour's time. Brittle smiling went on as everyone congratulated Germayn, the other contestants saying how much they'd enjoyed it as an experience. Hoping against hope the studio verdict was a fluke, that one of them may yet be up there.

Thousands of viewers, as well as ringing in to vote for Tartine, were asking about the doll. Of course the whole story came out then. Both public and tabloids were beguiled by Harriet's role in Germayn's success, the act based on the doll, the partnership between creator and performer.

Harriet had no alternative but to tell Alb before they went to Church the following day. By now all their friends, including Mr Coulson, via Tundra, knew of the problems at Number Nine. Harriet went out early and bought the papers, looking through them with Erica in her bedroom.

'It's fantastic. Your picture's in every one. You've done it, made your dream happen.'

'We were so busy working I can't believe it. It hasn't sunk in.' Harriet was incandescent with pleasure and apprehension.

'Better tell him before one of the neighbours does. Or Grandma rings,' her sister urged.

'He'll go bananas.'

'What else is new? He's already livid for half a dozen other reasons. Go for it, sis.'

'After breakfast.' Harriet's pale blue eyes distended with worry. 'I'll unplug the phone to stop callers till then.'

There was a strained silence at the table. None of them had much appetite sitting with Alb staring through them as he crunched toast and gave curt orders for more tea. As

Doris began clearing the table Harriet fetched the papers.

'Dad, I've something to show you.'

'What've you brought these rags into the house for? You know I don't allow them. Get them out. Now.'

'I want you to read this, about my new job.'

'Your what? You aren't changing jobs unless I say so, lad. There's nothing wrong with the one you've got. You told me it had prospects.'

'Read it, please.' Determined, she turned to the photos of the two Tartines posing with herself, the accompanying write-ups. The three women kept quite still, watching him. He blanched, staring in disbelief for several seconds. He jabbed the paper, glared at Harriet.

'You've done this, consorted with them behind my back? You've - you've done this thing with that creature's son? How dare you!'

'I hoped you'd be pleased for me.' Harriet was blatant, 'I've always wanted to work in showbiz, you know, and it's my big break.'

Alb rose to his feet, features contorted.

'Break? I'll give you a break!'

Leaping up he threw the papers across the room, except the *Sunday Times* which, at record speed, he rolled into a truncheon. Roaring, he lunged at Harriet who dashed into the hall, squeaking with alarm. She ran out the front door but, halfway down the path, looked back, poised for flight.

'Alb, leave her alone!' Doris screamed.

Erica grabbed the broom as a counter weapon while her father ran up and down the hall, furiously smashing pictures off the walls, smithereening a three dimentional plaque of Polperro.

'Defy me, would you?' he roared. 'Traitor! I won't tolerate a Judas in my house. Or any of your effigies!'

With that he dived upstairs. Harriet came back to hover in the doorway, see what he would do. To her dismay he barged into the forbidden territory of her bedroom, reappeared with fistfulls of teendolls.

'No, don't touch them!' shrieked Harriet.

'You and these things - out!' bawled Alb, pelting her with them.

She, Erica and Doris tried to catch the missiles as they flew in all directions.

'My girls, my girls!' Harriet wailed, scooping them up.

Alb thundered back upstairs, returned with more. Wielding a clump of Barbies like a club he bore down on Harriet, hitting at her. Clutching those she'd retrieved she ran out of the drive and up the side of the Tylers' house. Germayn and Tundra, cooking breakfast as they also perused the papers, looked up.

Incensed though he was, Alb couldn't bring himself to set foot on their territory. He stood at the gate, mucus flecking the edge of his mouth as he banged the Barbies' heads against the gate.

'Phew,' said Germayn, coming out, 'he's really lost it.'

As Harriet gave a tearful account to them her father ran back into Number Nine. A minute later the back bedroom window crashed open and he leaned out.

'Take your graven images. Take your false idols!' he bawled, lobbing teendolls into next door.

Germayn and Harriet ran round the lawn, fielding them as they flew over the hedge like a plague of stiff-limbed fairies, lodging in trees and flower beds. When the Lilliputian victims had been collected and stacked Germayn brought a large box for them.

'Are they all here?'

'Most of them. I'll get the rest when he's out. If he doesn't destroy them from spite.'

'Lucky the Tartine doll's in our front room,' Germayn gave a whistle of relief. 'She's vital for our publicity.'

Harriet was shaken.

'You'll stay with us, darling.' Tundra said as they listened to Alb through the hedge, berating Doris.

'Call yourself a mother?' he was bawling. 'Call yourself respectable? You've condoned this business behind my back all along. You aren't fit to be my wife. Do you hear?'

He wanted to grab her hair, throw her to the floor to show her he wouldn't be defied, but Erica, holding the broom at the ready, stood beside her mother with a watchful scowl. The taste of bile was in his throat. He struggled to think of a punishment.

'From now on I won't lower myself to speak to you,' he said.

'Yippee!' cheered Casey as he turned his back on Doris and Erica and stormed to the greenhouse.

Next door Germayn pulled a wry face at his mother but Harriet excused herself and ran to the bathroom.

'Poor lass. That twerp tries to spoil everything,' said Tundra, 'but she'll forget him when you two get stuck into your careers.'

After the show last night there was a flurry of offers, initially for TV and radio interviews. But the big agency's rep stepped up to stake his claim. He'd talked of Blackpool, of summer shows, of panto, and they had an appointment at his office next week.

Tundra reminded her son that along with an agent he needed a personal manager. 'Someone who'll look after your interests, who's organised, and that's Harriet. You'll come to an arrangement with her in any case. She created Tartine so she owns the copyright.'

'Mumzo, we discussed it weeks ago. We're having a contract drawn up for our partnership.'

As she washed the breakfast dishes Erica was also glad for Harriet. Now her sister had found a way out she supposed she'd eventually get a flat, a life. With a bit of luck she herself would be next. But what about poor Mum?

Over tea and biscuits after church, defiantly attended by Harriet, flanked by her friends, the Wakes' and Tylers were a hub of attraction. Dreamstars was watched by most of

St. Chad's congregation who'd also seen the Sunday papers. Struggling his way out of the handshaking, exclaiming and back-slapping, wearing a fixed grin, Alb thought he would bite the next person who congratulated him on being Harriet's father. It was his mother. When he got home Lily rang, simpering with pride, to take credit for the fact Our Harriet was so clever. But of course everyone knew she took after her grandmother who was noted for her skill at sewing and organising people. And that Tartine Zircon was so good, wasn't she? You'd never think it was a chap. When Alb went into work on Monday everyone in Tool Magic was agog to hear about Harriet and Germayn. There was no escape.

He couldn't retract his vow of silence towards Doris without losing face and the following week she made sure food and fresh clothes were presented to him as usual with no word exchanged. Each evening after the meal she disappeared next door with Erica. He heard snatches of their conversation with the Tylers till late. When they came home he listened for Doris going into the back room where she was using Bernardine's old bed.

Emptied of people, Number Nine had a hollow sound. Being there alone made him uneasy and playing music merely emphasized the silence behind it. He went round straightening furniture and cushions, continually tidying. He even ventured into the back bedroom, starkly bare with its rows of empty niches and drawers, Doris having taken Harriet's remaining things to her. It wasn't possible for him to spend time at the church hall as the contractors were in, starting alterations. He couldn't even ask neighbours if they needed anything doing as Dreamstars came up every time they met him.

He eased his jitters by gardening but it was haphazard, disjointed, with nobody for him to give orders to. It was bitter satisfaction to root out the remaining blackcurrant bushes, dig up flowerbeds, anything planted by that deviant Bernard, so the area became a series of craters. Towards the end of the week he was in the front garden so couldn't dash away, when Tundra and the vicar came up the path, Mr Coulson carrying catalogues.

'Evening, Albert. I'm glad we caught you.'

Alb bridled at the words. 'I've got information from the sound and lighting firms we talked of. May we come in?'

Alb wanted to shout, 'you, yes. But I won't have that monster over my threshold!' He muttered, 'please do.'

With every stride she took into the house it seemed Tundra was conquering it, taking him hostage. Each time he saw her she seemed to grow larger, more menacing. She and Mr Coulson wore cheery expressions and there was something obvious about the way they made no mention of hurtling dolls. They sat at the table discussing the different rigs' suitability for the venue. Tundra clapped a hand on Alb's shoulder to make a point. He felt it was like being hit with a ham.

'I taught sound and lighting on my drama course and I've been the tech person for dozens of student shows. I'll familiarize you with the desk we're getting, though this is updated from when I used it.' She pointed to the photo, 'once it's installed we'll try the new refinements together.'

'Tundra's an excellent teacher,' the vicar nodded. 'Actually, we can go now and see what they're doing at the hall.'

Alb had no reason to refuse. They went in her car and he felt usurped when the vicar sat in the passenger seat and he had to get in the back.

The hall was a mess of brick dust and scaffolding with men in safety hats knocking through walls but the entrance was relatively clear. In the vestibule the vicar led the way up a flight of stairs to the old lighting box. Used for years as a storeroom, but now cleared of junk, it was revealed as a large space. A breeze block wall was in the process of construction at one end. Alb felt a flicker of interest.

'That will be a cupboard for equipment, extra lamps and mics,' said Tundra. 'Then there'll be a built-in bench running along here for your light and sound desks.' She indicated the large window overlooking the stage and auditorium. As she pointed with one hand she rested the other on him a moment, causing him the shrinkage he'd experienced at their first meeting. She spoke in her measured, cordial manner but he knew it was her fault his family had turned against him. They'd hatched plots to undermine him because of her.

'It'll be a first rate little theatre.' Mr Coulson leaned through the window, regarding the hall. 'A pity to spoil all that painting you and the girls did, Alb. But there's no point in delay when we're blessed with such funds. Oh, the Lord's been munificent!' He clapped his hands. 'D'you think Germayn will do the honours on opening night, as our local celebrity, Tundra?'

'I'll make sure of it.' She turned to Alb. 'Which reminds me, you're invited to the celebration I'm throwing for him and Harriet on Saturday.'

'Can't make it, thanks all the same. It's my evening to visit my elderly mother. I couldn't let her down. Looks forward to seeing me.'

'Harriet's grandma? She's coming with your brother so you can see her here. We expect all the Wakes family.'

They'd blocked his escape routes. If he feigned illness George and his mother would have to know. Mother would tell him to pull himself together the way she did when they were children. She refused to tolerate sickness and when they contracted chickenpox or mumps they collapsed where they stood before she'd allow them bed or doctor.

Perversely part of him wanted to attend the party. Missing such a public event where he would still be part of the glory, even reflected from that gormless lad of his, went against his nature. But loathing of Tundra overrode every other consideration and his hatred squirmed in him, a nest of maggots. He wouldn't go.

On Saturday he returned from the supermarket after walking round it with a depleted List, which he'd had to tick off himself. He was also having to open the carport gates, as Doris was nowhere to be seen, when Mr Couslon's rosy snout appeared above the hedge.

'Albert, that's lucky. Just the man we need.'

The magnetic phrase had its usual effect. Alb paused from unloading bags.

'Can we impose on your kindness yet again? I'm having difficulty fixing the party lights.'

Alb wanted to refuse. He hadn't ventured on to Tyler territory since that initial meeting with Tundra and her son. His scalp pricked as he followed the vicar. Germayn had just finished cutting the back lawn and was scraping the mower blades as Harriet emptied clippings on the compost heap. They looked towards him but said nothing and he kept his back to them. From the stepladder he could see into the Tylers' kitchen. Erica was rolling pastry as Doris took a tray of buns from the oven. She'd better be home in time to make his lunch or there'd be trouble, he scowled.

As he necklaced the trees with coloured bulbs the vicar passed him, and checked wiring, the thought hit him, Rick and Harry were quite capable of doing it. The business about the theatre, and now this, he'd been asked in case he felt left out. He was being patronised! Him! Alb Wakes, who the whole neighbourhood looked up to.

'Two sugars for you, isn't it, Alb?' Tundra had brought them coffee.

Was there anything she didn't know about him? He took a token mouthful, burning his tongue as he glared after her retreating back. As if to confirm it, the Norfax manager arrived and went into the kitchen with her. Alb threw the rest of the coffee on the ground and said he must be going.

'I'll see you later then,' said Mr Coulson.

'Tundra's right, Mum. You may as well strike while he's still gob-smacked about the contest, get it over with,' said Erica as they watched Alb hurry past the kitchen window.

She'd just been let into the secret about the car. At Tundra's suggestion Mr McCloud was to bring it to the Close that evening for the revelation.

'But,' said Doris, 'what if he - '

'He won't dare, in front of everyone. Couldn't stand denting his image.'

That evening found Alb sitting in Tundra's front room, reluctantly sipping beer and making small talk with the neighbours, who went on interminably about the contest. She had invited just about everyone in the Close, plus dozens of other guests. The doorbell rang constantly as yet another turned up carrying plates and bottles. There were artist friends of hers, musicians, a film actor who turned out to be her godson, plus the Norfax manager. The glamour of the drag queens from Saucy Girls made everyone else look dowdy, except for Tundra herself, garbed in a green robe of operatic proportion.

But the star of the evening had to be Germayn. His appearance gave Harriet a glow of creative pride. She'd sat over the sewing machine throughout two nights making that gown but it beat dressing teendolls any day. He was, however, closely rivalled by a young couple with fountains of blonde hair, biker mates of his. Norry arrived with Sue, his heavily pregnant wife, crammed in the sidecar. He was resplendent in rubber miniskirt, fishnets and glitter platforms while Sue looked sensual in a thonged leather maternity dress with spike covered knee-boots. Erica's college friends were impressed. They hadn't known she mixed with such cool people.

Flex Tyler was in America with the Quartet, but his music was played to set the evening in motion. Then Clare and Darrel put on CDs they'd brought. As the perfumed mass began to rock Alb maneouvred himself into the garden. There was a large enough crowd for him to avoid any contact with his family, apart from his mother and brother.

But Lily and George greeted him briefly, intent on bagging celebrities. To Alb's chagrin, she didn't disguise her delight at being introduced to Germayn. An evening with Tartine Zircon was something worth boasting about to her cronies. He knew Doris and the others were deliberately keeping their distance from him. Shaun and Bernardine, tending the barbecue, behaved as if they'd never met him and didn't want to.

His glance was drawn again and again to Doris. He saw her whole aspect as calculated to insult him. Forbidden ever to appear in trousers she wore a pair that hung baggily from her thin rump. She seemed to have only her vest on over them and her hair was tied in a skimpy bun, no bigger than a conker. There, he was right. He'd known such a weak character would turn decadent at the first chance. For her own good, as a Christian woman he would regain control of her. He'd speak to her again when he felt she was punished enough by his silence. But not here. People were sitting or standing in groups, talking. Angrily he saw her laugh at what someone said. Laughing at him, no doubt!

He turned away and went cold at the sight of Tundra and Mr McCloud leaning on each other, swaying to the music, the Norfax manager's head resting on her collar bone, engulfed in a sleeve of her robe, like a contented animal peering from a thicket. Taking a tit-bit from his plate he fed it to her. Alb closed his eyes, quelling the hallucination that it wasn't a slice of quiche she ate, but his building society passbook.

It caused a loosening quiver in his bowels. Putting down his glass he negotiated the crowd, slipped behind the cherry tree, through the gap in the hedge. He thought they were all too preoccupied to notice but the vicar saw him disappear into his garden.

When he came out of the bathroom the quiet of the house steadied him but the noise of the party beat across the Close, bouncing off walls. He went round, banging windows shut, then picked up the TV paper. He would lose himself in watching something. A detective mystery? No. A film? Ah, he'd marker-penned a documentary about the British Army. He switched on the set and sat down. A Grey snowstorm. He tried other channels, checked the leads. There was no reception.

Reluctantly he went outside, to the end of the garden, where he squinted against the setting sun at the aerial. It was attached to the chimney at the back of the house and leant at an odd angle. He wondered if last night's wind had caused damage. Fetching ladders he set the long, aluminum one against the house wall and went up it, pulling the wooden roof ladder after him. Reaching the top of the aluminum ladder he pulled the light wooden one in place, pushed it flat against the slates, until its hooks caught over the roof ridge. Feeling visible to the partygoers he glanced down but, apart from the high screen of hedge, everyone's attention was on a performance from the latest guests, a black acapella group.

Their deep, honeyed voices, the sad harmony of the song induced an attack of self pity. He saw Lily talking to some Saucy Girls. What did any of his relatives care about him? Too busy making fools of themselves. Mother would notice all right if he plunged off this roof. His death would be like Dad's, bringing her happiness when she collected the insurance. Every year she'd hold a day of remembrance for him as well as Dad. Maybe she'd combine the two. Alb had no intention of harming himself for anyone but toyed with the mournful idea. It vanished when he remembered the beneficiary on his policy was Mrs Doris Wakes. He'd get that changed.

On all fours, distributing his weight in order not to crack the slates, he climbed towards the leaning aerial. Holding on to the chimney stack with one hand he knelt, tried to grasp the aerial with the other. It seemed to be jammed. Cautiously he pulled himself up by one of the chimney pots.

The end of the song released waves of chatter which washed over him. The dense texture of the hedge seemed to surge and recede. The barbecue crackled and the smoke's greasy succulence drifted up, turning him nauseous. All the other times he'd been on the roof he'd never experienced this dizziness. He clutched at the chimney.

Something below caught his attention. It was Doris again. Dancing! He had never seen her dance in his life. She and the boss of Spraffy's were jigging incompetently round the patio. Alb wished for a machine gun. A grenade.

He stood up, about to break his vow and shout at her, when a huge violence jerked him sideways. He yelled, clawing the air, his feet wheeling as he half fell, half slid down the roof as the chimney pot and a shower of bricks rolled away from him. The pot caught the aluminum ladder, knocking it to the ground, then itself smashed into a bush.

'Did you hear a crash?' Erica asked Gareth as they nibbled vol au vents.

He shook his head, 'they've probably dropped something in the kitchen. You've done a great job with these.'

Alb, his knees grazed, clung to the wooden ladder and scrabbled himself back on the roof ridge, He sat, shaken, not just by his near miss but also the fact he'd been ignorant of a serious fault in his house. What if this had happened when the window cleaner was here and the pot killed him? Alb, in whose family falls had such resonance, saw himself sued for all he'd got. He wondered what to do next.

There was no way he was going to draw attention to himself, call for help. He could just see that lot laughing at his expense. He would wedge himself behind the stack, quietly try to stay hidden till Doris came home, then attract her attention and make her retrieve the ladder. He needn't speak to her after that. Hugging the back of the chimney, knees bent, he splayed his feet so his shoes acted as chocks to prevent himself sliding down the slates and pressing his nethers against the brickwork. He settled for a long, furious wait.

Erica thought how beautiful the Tylers' garden looked as night began to fall. Candles and Chinese lanterns, lights in the trees, figures swaying to a slow number. She and Gareth moved dreamily, heads resting against necks as they horse-nuzzled each other.

'This is the best party. Not that I've been to many.'

'It is. But it's nearly midnight so we must leave the ball, Cinders.'

'What d'you mean?'

'I've a better one arranged. Strictly for you and me. I've got Dad's car down the road.'

'Where are we going?'

'Gran's. I've even got champagne chilling in her fridge.'

'You're kidding. The last thing I need now is a cookery lesson.'

'Not tonight. She rang earlier to say she arrived safely in Tenerife.'

'Oh.' Excitement gripped her. She looked round. Nobody would notice if they left. Her glance fell on Doris, 'I'll leave a message for Harriet to pass on to Mum.'

Doris, strings of party popper in her hair, was amongst the revellers dancing a conga round the Close, too occupied having fun to notice her daughter and Gareth glide down the street.

He parked in the road parallel to his grandmother's and they crept in the back gate, entered the house without switching on lights to hide their presence. He collected a bottle from the fridge and as its coldness brushed her arm Erica shivered. Hand in hand they crossed the shadowed kitchen. The headlamps of a passing car flared blue through cornflowers in the hall door as they padded upstairs. Three closed doors on the landing. She knew the bathroom from her previous visits. Gareth opened one of the others.

'We're not, I mean, we're not in your Gran's bed?'

'Front room. Kept exclusively for visitors, which we are, unofficially.'

In the dark room the outline of the window showed

faintly through closed curtains. She made out the shape of a double bed.

'I put these ready.' He lit candles.

Erica turned to look at herself, then him, in the dim pool of the dressing table mirror as he sat on the bed, removing trainers and socks. She remained standing, slowly slipping out of her shoes, watching him pull off trousers and shirt, throw them into a corner.

Wearing only trunks he stood up, lifting the weight of hair from her shoulders to kiss them. She held her breath, pressing her palms over his chest as he ran a finger down her inner thigh, up under her skirt. She sighed, raised her arms as he ballooned the dress over her head. Remembering, he turned to the bottle on the bedside table. 'Stand clear.'

She covered her ears as the cork shot out. 'Gosh. Extravagant or what?'

'Scrounged off my dad, who was given it by a client.'

Fizz bubbled down the bottle neck, wetting his arms, spittling her legs as he filled glasses. They clinked, 'to us.'

In spite of the gold that foamed her senses, she was paralyzed with nerves. Ridiculous, someone her age being scared to do it when she fancied him rotten. She should have reached this point years ago. Been well in practice by now. As they stood draining their glasses she noticed the boxes. Dozens of them, stacked on the dressing table, the floor, a chair.

'What on earth are those?'

'Gran's present hoard.'

'What?'

'It's been here as long as I can remember. Look.' He passed her boxed soaps, talc, brush-and-comb sets, a coffee percolator, slippers. He opened the wardrobe to reveal more, piled on shelves. 'Every time she's given something for her birthday or Christmas it's put in here. Then recycled as a gift to one of her mates. They do the same.'

'So there's this collection of stuff constantly making the

rounds?'

'Yeah. Unopened for all eternity.'

Their laughter broke the tension. He poured refills, put an arm round her.

'I'm not getting drunk.' Her voice became small.

'I don't want you to.'

Taking her glass he placed it with his on the table, pushed her gently to the bed. The satin coverlet was cool against her back. The touch of his mouth made her want to laugh and cry simultaneously. With eager haste they tugged at underwear, peeling it from each other like fruit skin as night and the city floated away.

CHAPTER FIFTEEN

'He's having a sulk, Jeff,' said Tundra. 'Let him be.'

The vicar was concerned, 'But he went home hours ago, with a face like thunder.'

'His normal expression.'

'It's dark yet there aren't lights on. I'll check if everything's okay.'

Mr Coulson stepped through the hedge and saw the whole house in darkness. Had Alb gone to bed? Should he knock? Then he saw the ladder lying on the lawn. Such untidiness was odd in his churchwarden.

Surely he wasn't on the roof? Mr Coulson squinted up in the dusk then put the ladder against the wall and began climbing. At that same moment Tundra decided it was time to let off the fireworks. Germayn, standing chatting at the bottom of his mother's garden, looked upwards to watch and spotted a hunched gargoyle silhouetted against the sky behind the chimney.

'Oh my God, look!' he said to Harriet and Norry. 'Is he stuck?'

'Nah. You know what he's up to, don't you?' Norry was dismissive. 'He's going to try and ruin your party by threatening to jump. I was once with a girl who tried that trick every time I looked at anyone else.'

'He wants to get back at us. At me.' Harriet was afraid. 'But it would destroy Mum if he does. What can we do?'

'Spike his guns,' Germayn decided. 'He's only angling for attention. We'll make sure he gets it.' He went to the phone and dialled.

As Mr Coulson reached the top of the ladder and saw Alb, he realised he had positioned it in the wrong place, several feet along from the roof ladder. He called out to the crouching figure.

'Albert, it's only me, Jeff.'

Unwilling to accept rescue in this form, Alb was

dumbstruck with embarrassment. They eyed each other in the reflected light from next door. The vicar had twice had the experience of talking down potential suicides, one a man dumped by his girl, the other a disappointed Manchester City fan threatening to hang himself with a scarf when relegation threatened.

'This isn't the way for us to solve your problem,' he coaxed. 'You know I'm your friend?'

'Look, I don't want them to find out,' said Alb, referring to his being trapped.

'Why don't I move the ladder and you can come down and we'll discuss the problem in confidence. Just the two of us.'

'You don't understand.' Even though he had contemplated ending it all for a brief moment, Alb was affronted, realising the vicar's meaning. How could he believe Alb would destroy someone as valuable as himself. He shouted above the bangs from next door, 'there's nothing to discuss. It was the pot -'

Another firework exploded. The vicar raised his eyebrows. Pot. Who'd have thought it? Alb, the picture of respectability, the one who sat in judgement on the rest of them. He himself had left such things behind in his youth.

'Just a bit of weed was it, Alb?' Mr Coulson wanted to make sure.

Deafened by the noise Alb glared at him, 'Wee...? No I don't need to. I came up to fix the aerial and - ' His words were obliterated in a shower of stars, '- next minute I was sent flying.'

'Flying.' The vicar caught the end of the sentence, 'I see.'

More serious than the odd spliff then? That wouldn't have driven him up here. Speed. If he'd taken that his perception of danger must be altered. Careful handling was needed to get him down, avoid a tragedy.

'I'm coming to join you.' Bravely, the vicar decided physical contact was called for and began to crawl on to the roof.

'No, don't!' cried Alb, thinking of damage to his tiles as well as his pride. 'Keep back! It could be loose.' A rocket zapped past them.

'I'm only coming to talk.'

'D'you want to be killed?'

Mr Coulson retreated. What did he mean? Had it sent him into in a murderous state? Drugs would certainly explain some of Alb's behaviour as reported to him by Tundra.

'It's falling apart,' repeated Alb, above the sound of the rocket's disintegration.

'We often feel that way,' the vicar shouted back, 'but when we pray for guidance we - '

Over the loud music there was a commotion on the street side of the house as a fire engine sped up the Close.

'Ten minutes to get here. Those boys are super,' said Germayn.

Alb, edging up to lean over the roof ridge was mortified to see the crew jump out and look up at him, along with all the party guests who streamed out, glasses in hands, necks craning.

'Get back!' he screamed, in a sudden fury. If bits of chimney fell on that lot it spelt financial ruin.

'Do be careful. I think he's dangerous.' Germayn fluttered eyelashes at one of the crew.

A robot arm was unfolded from the engine and a fireman on the end rose towards Alb, calling, 'it's all right, mate. Don't move.'

'I think the chimney stack might collapse that side,' yelled Alb, pointing to the back of the house.

Mr Coulson, grasping the situation at last, descended the ladder in haste as the arm came across the roof, stopped by the chimney. Alb stood up unwillingly and was guided on to the platform by the fireman. A cheer rose as they sank towards the ground to flashing cameras, hastily grabbed by neighbours from their homes.

As he stepped out, mobbed with questions, prods, lights

trained on him, Alb was puce. He snapped out an explanation to the officer in charge then said he must go and set up a barrier in the back garden in case of further falling bricks.

'On Monday I'll contact a builder and my insurance firm.'

'Let us give you a hand, Alb.' Mr Coulson had popped through the hedge.

'Please. All go back to your gathering. It's terribly kind of you but it's just a domestic accident. I can manage.' He tried to be nonchalant.

Then Doris pushed through the crowd. 'Alb, are you really all right?'

Something had been waiting to snap in him. Forgetting his public face he turned on her, 'no! This is your fault, woman. You dragged us down with the wrong crowd and destroyed the family. You're getting out of it, right now!' He grabbed her arm and began pulling her across the pavement towards their house.

'Stop it!' Instead of submitting she struggled. He held her tighter and she raked her nails down his arm, leaving red scratches.

'That's quite enough. Hands off her!' roared Tundra, her huge grip closing on his collar. He tried to ward her off, flailing with one arm. Then he let go of Doris and turned to face his enemy, the onlookers frowning, amazed. He clenched his fists, as if to hit her. Everyone gasped. Germayn's skirt belled as he leapt to his mother's defence.

'Keep out of my business. I've had enough of your interfering. This is my wife,' screeched Alb.

'But not your property!' Tundra whirled Doris behind her.

'Get out of my way!' He tried to push Tundra aside. She gave him an almost playful slap in the chest which sent him staggering back. Two of the neighbours secured his arms and set him upright.

'Come now, Alb. You've had an upsetting experience but this is no way to go on,' the vicar said.

'Bloody vampire, that's what she is,' wheezed Alb. 'Siphons the life out of you.' Another wave of hatred went through him. Breaking from his captors he threw himself at her. More men tried to intervene but she calmly caught his wrists and held him at arm's length. Like a hooked fish he thrashed about, straining to break free.

'Albert, control yourself!' It was Lily's outraged voice, 'you're making a show of us.'

'Please, Alb -' Doris began.

There was a sudden, loud cry and they all turned to see Sue collapse to the ground, Norry sank after her.

'Oh!' cried Sue, 'I've started!'

'Oh!' cried Norry, 'you can't have. It isn't until next week. What'll I do?'

'Don't panic!' screamed Sue.

'I'm not!' screamed Norry. He knelt beside her, his face drained.

'I'll call an ambulance,' said Germayn.

'I just know it's going to happen soon.' Sue looked pleadingly at the ring of faces.

'It might be quicker if one of us drives her there,' Tundra decided. 'Unfortunately I've had a drop too much.'

A quick poll showed most guests were over the limit. Even those chauffeuring the others had imbibed a few measures.

'Nobody with alcohol in them is driving my wife and child,' Norry declared.

'I don't drink,' said Doris, 'I'll take you.'

'It's parked at the end, Doris.' Mr McCloud passed her the keys.

'As it's an emergency we'll escort you through town, clear your way,' said the fire officer.

Alb could not immediately escape through the press of people behind him and now paused, gaping, as she went down the Close and a moment later reversed a red car up to the gate. His altercation with Tundra was forgotten as people concentrated on easing Sue into the back of the car.

Norry sat beside her, his painted eyebrows, arched with worry. The fire engine swung on to the main road, siren blaring.

Doris drove after it, watched by the whole company. This unsuspected ability in someone they all knew as a dithery little creature was astonishing. Harriet looked at Germayn, who shrugged. They both turned to Tundra.

'I'll explain later.' She raised her voice, 'Doris will ring from the hospital with any news. But there's nothing more for us to do except continue the party.'

Laughing, exclaiming, tut-tutting, everyone moved back into the Tylers'. The music began again.

Inside Number Nine Alb, drenched in humiliation, steadied himself against the wall. Delving into the sideboard he found alcohol left from Christmas. He wasn't much of a drinker but downed two glasses of sherry then took the bottle through to the darkness of the front room. Had he dreamed it? He rubbed the sore scratches on his hand. It was unbelievable. Doris had changed into someone entirely different from the woman he'd married. Driving! If he hadn't witnessed it... Suddenly he remembered the day he came out of the dentist's. She'd betrayed him, same as those lads. He knew who was behind it.

He had to put a shield between him and the worshippers of Baal he could still hear through closed windows. His kind of songs were what he needed. He put on a CD of Boxcar Willie but, unless he closed his eyes he was still aware of the party, the Close, the day's intolerable events. By a table lamp he looked through his music videos. Yes, one of Dolly Parton. That was better. He could forget everything as he watched her pretty face singing, just for him. She was looking directly at him. She was stepping out of the screen. She was in the room, shaking her head.

'Ah guess y'know y'all hev bin behavin' real trashy to yuh family, Albert.'

He jumped up, his legs unsteady, opened all the doors to the back garden, came back and ripped the television from its moorings. With hysterical gasps he staggered outside with it, threw it to the ground. A spade stood near one of the holes. He dug it deeper then flung the set into it. He shovelled earth until it was buried. Then jumped on it. Over and over.

Although Doris appeared perfectly controlled as she sped after the fire engine, her mind was in turmoil. She was both ashamed and relieved that Alb's public demonstration of rage revealed to everyone the true state of their marriage. But she hadn't intended demonstrating she could drive in quite this way.

'Don't worry,' Casey materialized in the passenger seat. 'You're doing fine.'

Although she could never imagine what Casey looked like, Doris always knew when she was there. Behind her Sue groaned. 'He's coming!'

'Breathe like they showed us in ante natal class. Come on, gal,' directed Norry tremulously. They both began energetic panting.

'Hurry - oof - please!' shouted Sue.

'Nearly there, my dears.' Doris wasn't as calm as she sounded. 'You'll be in St. Mary's in a few minutes.'

As the traffic stopped to let their procession sweep noisily through the lights she tried to adopt a conversational manner with her hooting, gasping passengers.

'You know it's a 'he' then?'

'From our scans.' Scared though he was, there was delight in Norry's reply, 'my son.'

'Our - oof! oof! - son,' his wife amended, indignant.

Doris managed to concentrate on the road while she talked.

'Chosen a name?'

'Galadriel Lucifer Harley Ramsbottom.'

'Unusual. Lovely.'

'We've already nicknamed him - oof! - Gad. Aaargh! There goes my waters. He's nearly here.'

'You've got those towels tucked under her, Norry?' Doris checked, feeling it was unworthy to consider Rosie's upholstery at such a time.

'He's coming for sure.' Sue tried to shout but hadn't enough breath.

'Hurry!' Norry cried.

The fire engine turned off Oxford Road and wailed to a halt past the hospital entrance. Doris turned into the car park where the medics were ready. A stretcher was wheeled to the car. It was too late.

In a mad rush Doris assisted the hospital staff to open the back of the car, fold the rear seats flat and rotate Sue with her head to the steering wheel. A doctor and midwife leaned in to attend to her. She gave one deep throated roar and Gad slid triumphantly into waiting hands as he gave a high pitched yell of his own. Norry burst into tears as the baby was laid for a moment on his mother's chest before the two of them were hastily wrapped and whisked into the safety of the building. Staff and patients looked up as Norry clopped along after them in his finery, weeping with relief. Before following them, Doris locked the car.

'Good job Rosie's a hatchback,' she smiled to Casey.

'You were splendid,' said Casey, then vanished.

She had to stay at the hospital a while longer, supporting Norry while his wife was checked over on the ward. Doris brought him coffee where he sat snuffling and shaking in the corridor, and used her hankie to clean off his smeared make-up before they went in to congratulate Sue. When the grandparents arrived Doris made it her cue to leave.

It was three in the morning as she drove back to Riffton through empty streets. It had been a stupendous night. Her whole personality felt rinsed out, cleansed. She was filled with elation, as though she too was newly born.

At Number Nine she went into the front bedroom where Alb lay clothed on top of the duvet, staring at the ceiling, something he had taken to doing.

'Alb, you have to stop this nonsense and speak to me.'

He made no response.

'Alb! There's something I have to discuss with you.'

He turned his head away, 'I've nothing to say to you, woman! Leave me alone'.

'No. I've things to say to you, whether you like it or not. For starters, there's my Rosie.'

Rosie. So that was her name. His face tightened but he didn't look at her. At last he bit out, 'a friend of that one's is she? Another worthless bitch like you? I don't care what you two get up to.'

Casey's voice came from Doris then. It was icy, 'of course I'm not worthless. And Rosie isn't a woman. She's my car.'

Now he stared, gave a sharp laugh. He was incredulous. 'Your car? Yours? That car belongs to you? Don't be stupid.'

Doris went to the window, pulled back the net, 'there, I've parked outside.'

He scowled a moment, then got up and looked out. 'That's never yours. How could you buy a car? You can't even buy a loaf properly.'

'I won it in a competition. In a women's magazine.'

There was a long pause. She saw him gulp, struggle with himself for a full minute.

'A competition. Huh! And what d'you think you're going to use this car for?'

'To take me to work. I've been there in it three times so far.'

He actually stumbled, put a hand against the wall to steady himself. He was more flabbergasted than when he first saw her drive.

'I've got a job as canteen assistant at Keggs Dell. I've only done a few shifts as it's near the holidays but they've promised me more next term.'

Tremors of rage went through him. He started to screech obscenities at her. She'd never heard him do that before. She wasn't afraid. It was like watching a barking dog.

'Listen, whore,' he finally hissed, 'what those lads did was bad enough, but you! This piece of stupidity means you've done it once and for all! Cooked your goose, signed your death warrant, woman! I'm divorcing you!'

'Fine!' said Casey in her head.

'Fine!' echoed Doris. She folded her arms, looked straight at him.

'I mean it. I'm not bluffing, woman!'

'Me neither.'

'D'you understand? I'm kicking you out. You'll be homeless. You won't survive five minutes when I throw you on the street.'

'I won't be there, Alb.' Casey fed the words and Doris repeated them. Calmly she picked up her handbag, checked her keys. 'The court will award me half the value of whatever this place fetches when it's sold.'

'Sold...? Nobody's selling my house.' The woman was totally mad. She was making it up. Number Nine belonged to him. She belonged to him. He was the one to decide what happened to them. She went downstairs, closing the front door quietly after her. From the window he watched her get in the car and drive away.

His mind went into a state of white-out. Everything that had been effective for him in the past no longer worked. All life's signs and instructions were now in a foreign language. There was a hammering in his head.

The breeze rushing through the open window was warm, carrying summer scents, dawn streaking the sky as Doris put her foot down, driving into the Cheshire countryside. She hadn't been for a spin by herself to savour the sheer pleasure of it before.

'I did it, Casey. Anything's possible now, don't you think?'

203

She waited for the voice to reply, for the familiar dialogue in which she was advised, admonished, congratulated. 'Casey?' She said it loudly several times but there was no answer. Then she knew. I don't need you any more. Thanks, Casey, and goodbye, she thought. And as she drove she laughed long and loud, the wind in her hair.